FETLOCK[S]

The Curse of the Pony Vampires

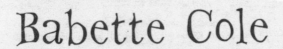

Babette Cole

BLOOMSBURY

LONDON BERLIN NEW YORK SYDNEY

Bloomsbury Publishing, London, Berlin, New York and Sydney

First published in Great Britain in June 2011 by Bloomsbury Publishing Plc
36 Soho Square, London, W1D 3QY

A CIP catalogue record of this book is available from the British Library

ISBN 978 0 7475 9933 3

Typeset by Hewer Text UK Ltd, Edinburgh
Printed in Great Britain by Clays Ltd, St Ives Plc, Bungay, Suffolk

1 3 5 7 9 10 8 6 4 2

www.babette-cole.com
www.bloomsbury.com

To
Flanagan

Rogues Gallery

Arabella & Antonia
Fitznicely

Lord Walter Fitznicely

Lady Sarah Fitznicely

Sir Faustus
Fangley-Fitznicely

Morriati and Mercedes
Fangley-Fitznicely

Countess Mortia-Antoinett
Fangley-Fitznicely

Ben Faloon

Potty Smythe

Henrietta
Wellington-Green

Dominic Trelawney

Matt Khareef

Bunty Bevan

Peter Fixcannon

Carlos Cavello

Gilly Jumpwell

Philippa
Horsington-Charmers

Sam Hedges

CHAPTER ONE

The Unwelcome Intrusion

Penny was riding Patch in the orchard behind
the farm at Fetlocks Hall. It was late May and
the apple trees were in full bloom.

It was the perfect day. The sun shone in a
bright blue cloudless sky, making dappled shadows
beneath the trees and giving a glossy shine to her
pony's coat.

Penny gave Patch a hug around his brown and white neck.

'Patch,' she said, 'who'd ever have thought, at ten years old, I'd be lucky enough to get a scholarship to a magical pony school like Fetlocks Hall and have you as my friend?'

'And who'd have thought I'd be the luckiest pony in the world to have a real Unicorn Princess like you as mine?' he replied. 'Someone who could speak to me like this in Equalese, teach me to fly, dance and take me on exciting adventures.'

'Yes – wasn't it great when we went to Equitopia to meet the Unicorns for my coronation by King Valentine Silverwings?' Penny continued. 'If he hadn't given me my special Unicorn Princess powers and my Lance of Courage, Queen Starlight's Horn and the vial of Unicorn Tears, we'd never have defeated those nasty red, scaly Devliped ponies and stopped them stealing the Equilibrium of Goodness.'

'I've never really understood what that is, you know,' confessed Patch.

'Well,' said Princess Penny, 'it's a set of mythical scales that maintains the balance between Good and Evil. It's the Unicorns' job to keep the scales carefully balanced on the Goodness side. If it tips the other way our world of Terrestequinus and Equitopia would be horrible places for us all to live in. The Devlipeds want to steal the scales and get control of them. They plan to make our two worlds as evil as theirs. It's my duty as a Unicorn Princess to defend these scales and protect them and all of us from the Devlipeds, who want to take over the school and turn it into one that teaches wicked children to help them steal the scales. Fetlocks is an important place to the S.U.S. (Secret Unicorn Society). Our head-mistress has to run it as a school for especially gifted equichildren to develop their magical pony skills. Fetlocks A students help the Unicorns protect the scales. That's why King Despot Dragontail, King of the Devlipeds, hates the school and will do all he can to get it closed down or at least stop it running in its usual way.'

'Phew! Lucky Fetlocks to have its own Unicorn Princess,' said Patch.

The sun was quite hot now so Penny steered her pony into the shade of a big tree. She slipped off his back to give him a rest and some grass to eat.

'I could not have done anything without your help, Patch,' she said, stroking his neck as he munched the grass, 'or the Fitznicelys – Lady Sarah,

Sir Walter, and Arabella and Antonia. It's just as well only Potty Smythe, the dogs, you ponies and I can see them,' she continued. 'Arabella and Antonia get up to some funny pranks and some of their habits are a bit scary, but they're useful spies and strong supporters of our team.'

Patch flicked his tail and pricked his ears. 'The other ponies and I love being in our team! The Fetlocks Hall Flyers sounds really cool, doesn't it?'

'Yeah,' beamed Penny, picturing her special school chums and team members. 'Pip, Sam, Carlos, Matt and Dom are just the best, aren't they?'

Patch nodded and nuzzled her nose.

Penny thought how peaceful it was in the orchard that day with her pony, the sunshine, the smell of the sweet grass and the pretty pink apple blossom. She hoped the Devlipeds would never come back to Terrestequinus to disturb it.

But that was all to change.

As she sat dreaming under the tree a shower of pink and white apple blossom whipped up like a whirlwind. Patch snorted as the cloud of petals blew towards them.

Penny stood up. Her heart was beating fast. Both of them were unsure what this strange occurrence meant but all became clear as Penny made out the shape of a beautiful Unicorn forming within the whirling petals.

Valentine Silverwings, King of the Unicorns, stepped out of the cloud. This looked like Secret Unicorn Society business.

'Good morning, Princess Penny,' said the King, walking over and rubbing his velvety nose on her cheek.

'Good morning, Your Majesty,' she replied, making a graceful curtsy.

'I'm afraid it's not as peaceful as you were hoping, my child,' he sighed, having read her recent thoughts. 'I've come to warn you about more disgusting Devliped skulduggery,' he said. 'Fetlocks Hall is going to need your help. I have a notion that they are plotting something to get rid of the school. Our brave little Irish brothers, the Ballycorns, sneaked into Devlipeditos through a hole in a peat bog in Cork. They sent me this information they recorded by telepathy.'

With that he blew a cloud of silvery air out of his nostrils. This formed a bubble in which Penny could see Despot Dragontail striding up and down in front of his generals, swishing his stumpy red scaly tail and blowing black sooty smoke out of his nose.

'I've had enough of Fetlocks Hall and that little witch Penny Simms,' he snorted. 'It's high time we got rid of that goody-goody school. Who wants to know about fairness and goodness and all that rubbish when it's stopping us from getting our way? I've thought of a cunning plan to get the place closed down or at least stop it functioning so that it can't turn out A students. They only strengthen the power of the S.U.S. and stop us getting hold of those wretched scales.'

'What's the plan, Your Majesty?' asked General Firespavin.

'Ah ha!' laughed the Devliped King. 'I've sent an anonymous letter to an organisation in charge of inspecting schools for Health and Safety and academic study to tell them a few things about that dump. I've said it's time it was inspected and closed down as it does not meet official standards. AND I've cursed the place with some batty friends of mine to help things into the bargain! Hee hee hee hee hee heee!'

Then he Catherine-wheeled out of the picture and a letter appeared in the bubble.

Penny gasped. Her eyes nearly popped out when she read the scrawly black writing.

Dear Office of Government Regulations
and Inspection of Boarding Schools (Ogribs),

You really ought to inspect an unruly,
dangerous school called Fetlocks Hall. It is
run by a lying, cheating headmistress called
Portia Manning-Smythe, who encourages
children in the practice of witchcraft.
The place is falling apart, unsafe for
respectable children and badly managed.
Pupils spend very little time at normal
school lessons because they are constantly
messing about with ponies and having a
good time. The headmistress lied about last
term's exam results because the academic
standard there is so low. The school is a
disgrace and should be closed down.

Anon.

'It's not true!' Penny exclaimed. 'We all work really hard at the lessons we *do* get. Fetlocks children are especially selected because we can learn quickly. We don't need as much time for school work as pupils at ordinary schools. Potty Smythe would never tell lies and she certainly wouldn't need to fib about our exam results! OK, so the Hall is a bit wobbly in places but the stable yard is what counts and that's as sound as a pound. No ponies are entirely safe, but if you know what you're doing and do as you're told there's little chance of an accident at Fetlocks.'

King Valentine Silverwings looked down his beautiful white nose at Penny and breathed in. The bubble disappeared.

'You're quite right, Penny,' agreed King Valentine. 'But I am not sure which of his nasty friends Despot Dragontail has asked to help him,' he sighed, 'Whoever they are there's bound to be trouble. Just keep a weather eye out for anything suspicious. Aunt Portia is going to need all your help here. I know I can trust you to do your best, Princess Penny, so I'm leaving it up to you. I'll be back in a few days for a report. Now kneel, child, and I'll give you my blessing.'

Penny knelt down in the pink petals. The King

gently tapped her on each shoulder with his beautiful golden horn.

'Arise, *Regina Electa*,' he breathed.

Penny stood up and he faded back into the apple-blossom cloud which floated up into the bright blue sky and disappeared.

'Oh dear,' said Patch, 'I don't like the sound of that.'

'We'd better warn the other ponies,' Penny said, climbing into her saddle. Together, they trotted back to the stable yard.

Penny had a difficult task ahead.

She couldn't tell her school chums about the Devliped curse as this was S.U.S. or Secret Unicorn Society business and highly secret. The Fitznicely family, Potty Smythe and the ponies could be told about the curse, but no one else. On the other hand, if OGRIBS were coming, everybody would have to know what to expect. That was school business and would not be secret at all. It was so hard to jump between the real and other-worldly aspects of Fetlocks Hall without spilling S.U.S. secrets (which Penny was bound to keep).

CHAPTER TWO

The Disgusting Problem

As Penny and Patch walked back into the stable yard under the archway with its ancient tower, the clock struck four. Carlos Cavello, one of Penny's special school friends, was riding around the yard on Budget, dribbling a polo ball between some upturned buckets with a long bamboo mallet. Budget had been a high-goal polo pony in her

10

day. She had scored many goals for her riders in the past but had retired to Fetlocks as a school pony. The two of them made it look very easy. Dom, Matt, Sam and Pip, Penny's fellow Fetlocks Hall Flyers teammates, were all watching the display. Finally Carlos struck the ball with his most powerful drive, the offside forehand. Penny watched the ball sail over the clock tower, the lawn and the great oak trees of the park to smash through the window of the headmistress's study in the great house. It landed in a very large mug of tea which Potty Smythe was about to drink.

'Nice shot, Carlos,' she called out of the broken window, mopping the tea off her blouse with a stable rubber.

Fishing the ball out of her mug, she turned her attention to the email from OGRIBS on her computer.

Dear Miss Manning-Smythe,
It has come to our attention that Fetlocks Hall is due for an inspection to ensure the school is adhering to our Health and Safety rules and regulations. Therefore Dr Sweepover and Mr Snoop, our inspectors from that branch of our office, will be paying you an official visit. We are also concerned about a letter sent to us

regarding false information given about last term's exam results. Therefore Dr Septimus Swottworm will also be visiting the school to test your pupils and teachers on their academic progress.

Potty Smythe looked worried. What was all this about? Health and Safety standards could never be the same at Fetlocks as any other school because it is a very unusual one where certain children's education is directed towards magical pony skills which are often very dangerous!

The headmistress was never one for red tape, rules and regulations. If OGRIBS imposed restrictions on Fetlocks it would be impossible to run it as a magical pony academy.

She was puzzled about the reference to the exam results. Fetlocks children were very bright and worked extremely hard at their lessons. The exam results were always good. Maybe someone somewhere was trying to get the school closed down by spreading horrid rumours implying she had somehow 'cooked the books!' by not telling the truth. She took a gulp of what was left of her tea and picked a bit of straw out of the computer keyboard.

* * *

Back on the stable yard everybody applauded Carlos's shot. He'd been playing polo since he was ten years old back home in Brazil and now had the idea of forming a Fetlocks Hall Flyers polo team. There was a suitable flat green field, big enough for a polo ground, in front of the main house. They had very game ponies who could turn a hoof to anything and enthusiastic riders who would make ace polo players. The rest of the Flyers were sold on the idea.

'What do you think, Pony Pen?' said Sam Hedges, the bravest of all Penny's friends. Sam was always up for a new adventure. She was a fearless rider and as courageous as her parents, who had been killed in a hunting accident. Potty Smythe had always thought she was excellent A student material.

'Sounds good to me,' Penny replied, dismounting from Patch, 'but as far as I know there are only four players in a polo team and there are six of us.'

'Then we'll find two more players and have two teams,' added Carlos. 'If we get good enough we can challenge other teams to matches.'

'Potty Smythe will love that,' said Pip. 'Polo is awfully smart and fashionable. A match would look really good on Open Day.'

'The Dubai Cup is the poshest match of all,' said Matt. 'My father's oil company sponsors it. I'm sure he wouldn't mind doing the same for us. We need mallets, helmets, visors, knee protectors, boots, breeches, polo shirts, posts and enough white boards to go around the polo ground.'

'Fantastic!' said Dom. 'Let's do it!'

Dom was not only a champion junior dressage rider with his fabulous pony, Sir Fin, but a really good surfer. He had been brought up by his surf instructor parents to meet any big wave that came along and never to turn down a challenge.

'A league of gentlemen salute, please,' said Carlos, dismounting.

They all formed a circle and piled their hands on top of each other's. Then they let out a loud view holla. When the cheering ended, they broke up the multi-storey hand pile.

Penny took off Patch's tack and walked him back to his field. He hadn't understood anything the other children were talking about so Penny explained to him about polo in Equalese.

'Polo is a fast, competitive, tactical game for teams of four riders on their ponies. It's played on a polo ground 300 yards long and 160 yards wide with twelve-inch high white boards round it to stop the ball going out of play too easily. At either end of the ground there are two goalposts eight yards apart.

'The game is divided into periods of play called chukkas. A full game has eight chukkas, but club matches have four or six. They last seven minutes each with three-minute intervals between each chukka and five minutes for half-time.

'Ponies have to gallop very fast all the time so they can only play two chukkas in a match with a rest of at least one chukka in between. Proper polo players have more than one pony – eight actually! The object of the game is to score goals, a bit like football. The team with the most goals wins the match.'

Patch said he liked the idea of polo but wasn't sure if he would be fast enough because his legs were so short.

'Come on, Patch,' said Penny, giving him a hug as she turned him out to join his friends in the home paddock. 'You're forgetting one thing. I'm a Unicorn Princess and I can do anything!'

'Can't wait to get started, then,' said Patch. 'I'll go and tell the other ponies about our new team and the latest Devliped developments.'

Penny gave him a mint from her pocket and unfastened his head collar, and he trotted off to tell his friends all the news.

* * *

As Penny walked back to the stable yard thinking over what King Valentine had shown her in the bubble and how she was going to have to tell Potty Smythe about the Devilpeds' sneaky plan, she noticed Arabella and Antonia Fitznicely, her twin ghostly friends and Unicorn Princess sisters, tearing towards her across the park in their side-saddles on their matching chestnut ponies.

They came to a screaming halt in front of her. Both twins looked very angry indeed.

'Oh, dear sister Penny,' gasped Arabella. 'Something quite horrid has happened to the mausoleum where we were buried! We are just on our way to tell Mama and Papa.'

'Come on,' said Antonia, offering her arm to Penny. She grabbed hold of it and the little ghost swung her up behind her side-saddle on Merryanzer. Penny instantly became as invisible as they were. She held on round Antonia's waist as they galloped towards the park railings, which they jumped, followed by a great leap down the ha-ha. Then they shot across the lawn towards the Ladies' Garden, where their mother, Lady Sarah, and their father, Sir Walter, were taking tea served from spooky teapots by their ghostly servants.

They pulled up sharply, making skid marks on the turf.

'Girls, girls,' gasped their father. 'Gently, please. The teacups are rattling enough to wake the dead!'

'Talking of the dead,' said Arabella, pulling Merryanzer away from a fallen apple fancy cake, 'have you seen our mausoleum recently?'

'Or smelt it?' chipped in Antonia.

'Don't be silly, dears,' said their mother. 'Our bodies have been dead for years – we can't possibly be smelly.'

'Mother,' said Antonia, 'there's a flock of disgusting pony vampire bats hanging out in there and the smell is appalling!'

'How absolutely revolting!' cried Lady Sarah, reaching for her smelling salts.

'This has probably got something to do with that unsuitable rogue, my half-brother Faustus!' raged Sir Walter.

'My dear,' said his wife, 'Faustus is a Veggipire and would never have encouraged any kind of *bloodsucking* vampires to come to Fetlocks.'

'He married one, you forget!' continued Sir Walter.

'But she is converted, is she not, my dear?' asked Lady Sarah, shaking out her fan and flicking it to and fro in front of her face.

'Of course she is, my love. He converted her to Veggipiredom with his beastly orange juice, that Fangley Zest stuff,' said Sir Walter, taking her hand.

'She may not be what she professes to be in other ways though.'

'I feel unwell,' said Lady Sarah. 'I shall return to my portrait until I am recovered.'

With that she evaporated into thin air.

'Mama always does that when Uncle Faustus's wife, the Countess Mortia-Antoinette, is mentioned,' said Arabella.

'It's because we think she isn't telling the truth about her title. She may have bought it or just made the whole thing up in order to marry into our family.'

'We have more urgent matters than family squabbles to attend to at the moment,' said Sir Walter. 'Now, Penny, do you know anything about these horrible pony vampires infesting our mausoleum in the woods?'

Penny looked aghast. She had no idea the Fitznicelys had a mausoleum at all. They had never mentioned it. She had heard about vampires, of course, but not the pony variety.

She thought carefully for a moment, remembering what King Valentine Silverwings had shown her in the orchard and the fact that Despot Dragontail said he had enlisted the help of some 'batty' friends to curse Fetlocks Hall.

She told the Fitznicelys about her meeting with

the King and his concerns for Fetlocks.

They went even paler than ghosts usually are.

'It must be so,' said Sir Walter, 'but why has Despot Dragontail sent them?'

Penny explained about the letter the King of the Devlipeds had sent to OGRIBS.

'Oh, my goodness!' said Arabella. 'We'd better tell Aunt Portia about it right now!'

'I was just on my way to let her know before you picked me up, but I'd like to see these pony vampire things for myself first,' said Penny.

The twins suggested she fetch Patch and they all go over to the mausoleum together. Patch came trotting over in response to her call.

Penny vaulted on to his back and Antonia and Arabella levitated behind her. When all three of them were safely on board the little pony, Penny said, '*Let's Fly!*'

Patch rose into the air and soared over the park towards the woods on the other side of Duns Copse. No one saw them because they were invisible when flying (or Equibatic as it is known).

There were broad rides between the trees that looked like leafy streets from the air. They all converged on a lonely dome-shaped building supported by pillars.

Patch thought it looked a bit creepy as he landed the girls at the bottom of the steps.

'Uggh!' said Penny, holding her nose. 'What an awful pong! Something smells as if it's been dead for a long time.'

'It's not us,' said the twins, opening the creaky door with a key hanging from a gargoyle.

It was dark and musty inside the mausoleum as they made their way down the dank steps to the crypt. Arabella lit a lamp so that Penny could see more clearly. It was really rather tidy down there with pretty painted marble tombs in neat rows. Each had reclining stone figures on them, some propped up on one hand in the 'toothache' position.

Arabella and Antonia floated over to a canopied resting place with two little cold marble girls lying side by side, hand in hand.

'Here we are,' said the twins.

Suddenly there was a horrible plop and a pile of orange droppings, big enough to belong to a small pony, sloshed on to the sleeping figures.

'Disgusting!' cried Arabella.

'Outrageous!' exclaimed Antonia, looking up at the ceiling.

There they were. Hanging up by their feet hooked over a beam, with their black wings wrapped around them and fast asleep, were dozens of pony vampires. They were about the size of a large African fruit bat. Their wingspan was about six metres and their furry bodies were the size of a mastiff or other large dog. It was hard to see their necks and heads as these were folded inside their wings, but Penny could make out two pony ears pointing towards the ground.

'They do smell terrible,' she said.

'It's their breath,' said Arabella.

'They have a pretty revolting diet of cow, sheep, pig . . . and, I'm afraid, pony blood!' added Antonia.

'I wonder if Uncle Faustus really does know anything about them,' said Arabella.

A shiver went down Penny's spine. She suddenly realised this was all part of the Devliped curse.

'Oh, my goodness,' she said. 'Obviously Despot Dragontail has sent the pony vampires to bite Terrestequines, our ponies, and turn them into pony vampires like them! They could be like every other pony and capable of nipping humans, who would then become vampires as well. No wonder he's enlisted their help. If all the ponies and humans at Fetlocks turn into vampires they'll be hunted down and killed! The school will cease to exist and there would be nothing to stop the pony vampires biting the Unicorns, who would probably turn into Vampirecorns! That would stop them from protecting the Equilibrium of Goodness because they themselves would be evil. It's another dastardly Devliped plot to steal the scales!'

'Yuck!' said Antonia and Arabella.

'Let's get out of here,' said Penny.

The three of them emerged from the vault, Penny blinking in the sunlight.

'What's down there?' asked Patch.

'You don't want to know,' answered Penny.

'I have to in case it's something rotten I have to warn the other ponies about,' he replied.

'Oh, they couldn't be more rotten,' said Penny . . . and she told him what she had seen and suspected about the Curse of the Pony Vampires.

Back in her study, or H.Q. as it was known, Potty Smythe was trying to reply to the email from OGRIBS when there was a knock on the door. She opened it to find Penny standing there with the Fitznicely twins hovering either side of her.

'There's a problem,' said Penny, looking sheepish.

'It's a DISGUSTING problem!' cried the twins.

'How dare Despot Dragontail send those revolting pony vampires here to stink out the place,' said Arabella.

'There's a flock of them hanging upside down in our mausoleum,' raged Antonia.

'They really are very smelly and have oodles of orange droppings,' said Penny, trying to stifle a giggle.

'Well, that's *really* going to look good when the Health and Safety bods turn up,' said the exasperated headmistress, slumping on to an old sofa and scattering the deerhounds and terriers who had been snoring on it.

She showed them the email from OGRIBS. Penny stared at it with her mouth wide open.

'King Valentine told me all about this in the orchard this morning,' she said.

'The Devlipeds are behind this and it was King Despot Dragontail himself who sent an anonymous letter to OGRIBS saying the school needed inspecting and that you had lied about our exam results.'

'Typical,' said Portia Manning-Smythe. 'I should have guessed he was behind it. I can't stop the inspectors coming now. Once OGRIBS get their teeth into something they're like a terrier with a rat. They won't let go. I'm going to need everyone's help here, especially yours, Penny.'

Penny suggested to the twins that their Uncle Faustus might be persuaded to help with the problem.

'Oh, come on,' said Arabella. 'He's a vegetarian

vampire, a complete wimp and has no respect for the dead!'

'That's probably because . . . well . . . I suppose, being a sort of a vampire, he isn't dead,' said Penny, 'but we've got to get rid of the pony vampires somehow. They're going to be real trouble when they wake up.'

'The whole thing is outrageous,' said Arabella.

'I think Papa is right,' said Antonia. 'It's something to do with Uncle Faustus . . .'

CHAPTER THREE

The
Fangley-Fitznicelys

Penny was intrigued with the Fitznicelys' attitude to the Fangley-Fitznicely part of their family. Nobody ever mentioned them. Sir Walter's half-brother, Faustus, was born to his father's second wife, Lilly Fangley. Little Walter had never liked her very much because she was an actress and a commoner until she married his father after his mother's death.

Faustus had adored his own mama, who kept pet bats in his nursery.

Faustus had been fascinated by bats since he was a small child in 1732. Sadly, a rather suspicious-looking one bit him when he was thirty. He could have been turned into a fully-fledged vampire except for the fact he was a vegetarian food scientist and organic gardener. He developed a special kind of blood orange called the Fangley Zest, which saved him from becoming a bloodsucker and freed him from the vampire curse.

Faustus was like a real vampire in every other way. He kept pet wolves and bats, slept in a coffin-shaped bed and disliked fire, crosses and garlic. He could turn himself into a bat or a wolf at will. His dark eyes were extremely sensitive to sunlight so he wore very thick sunglasses during the day. Like vampires, Veggipires cannot die unless someone sticks a stake through their heart. Nobody would ever want to do that as they are rather nice people, and so they never die – they are undead. Uncle Faustus was actually over 250 years old but he certainly did not look it. He, unlike his half-brother, Sir Walter, was completely visible to everyone and led a peaceful but rather sheltered life with his wife and two children in the Dower House to Fetlocks Hall.

His wife, Countess Mortia-Antoinette, had also been bitten by a vampire as a child in France. Secretly, she was closely related to the French Royal family. Poor little Mortia-Antoinette had been disowned by her father, the Count Belle Fontaine, because of her unfortunate accident. She had been sent to live with a simple shepherd and his wife in the Loire Valley. They did their best to keep the little teenage vampire Countess under control but she got free one night and pounced on Uncle Faustus, who was on a bat-finding expedition in that area in 1775. He converted her to Veggipiredom with his orange juice, fell in love with the stunning beauty and married her within a week.

The Fitznicelys never approved of the marriage. They refused to believe that Mortia-Antoinette was a real countess. One actress in the family was bad enough and a simple peasant from a shepherd's family posing as a countess was unacceptable! That was why the Fitznicelys had disowned the Fangley-Fitznicelys.

Uncle Faustus and his beautiful wife had two children: a son, Morriati, and a daughter, Mercedes. They were both born Veggipires and cousins to Arabella and Antonia, but the twins would never admit it.

They, like their parents, were just as visible to the living as they were to ghosts. Even though they were well over 200 years old they looked and behaved like modern children of eleven and twelve. However, they did look a bit eccentric but so did their parents in a very attractive way.

Penny was dead set on asking Uncle Faustus if he could help to get rid of the pony vampires. After all, he was a sort of vampire himself, even if he was a vegetarian one. She asked the twins if they would take her to wherever the Fangley-Fitznicelys lived.

'Oh no,' replied Arabella. 'We don't go there.'

'Mama and Papa wouldn't hear of it,' said Antonia, 'but you can find it yourself. They live in the Dower House. It's just beyond the mausoleum. Uncle Faustus is supposed to take care of it for us. That's why the crypt is cobweb-free and always has an oil lamp available for visitors.'

Penny said he couldn't have been there for a while or he would have seen the pony vampires.

'Oh, he probably has,' said Arabella. 'He'd be fascinated by them, being a bat lover. Best to go over there at dusk or night-time really. The Fangleys don't like the daylight much.'

Penny had never heard Potty Smythe mention Uncle Faustus and his family before, but she would have to ask for permission to visit the Dower House after dark. She found Potty in the hall on the telephone to Dr Septimus Swottworm, the academic inspector for OGRIBS.

'Dr Swottworm,' Potty was saying, 'I'm sure you will find that our Fetlocks children have a very high learning capacity and are progressing extremely well. In fact we only take children with an outstanding performance record because of the nature of our work here. I don't know where you got the idea that last term's exam results were not accurate. Yes . . . yes . . . I completely understand. Please let me know when you intend to visit. Thank you. Goodbye.'

She replaced the receiver and plonked into a chair with her head in her hands.

Penny told her of her plan to visit Uncle Faustus to seek his help and asked why the headmistress had never mentioned him before.

Potty explained that she'd never spoken about him or the rest of his family because it upset Lady Sarah terribly.

'She has been known to take to her portrait and not come out haunting for days at the very mention of them . . . but do go over to the Dower House tonight and ask Faustus if there is anything he can do. He'll have to act quickly though as we don't exactly know when the inspectors are likely to arrive.

OGRIBS give you little or no warning because they mean to catch you unawares.'

After dark Penny went down to the stable yard to fetch Patch. They flew over the treetops back towards the mausoleum. It was hard to find the Dower House because it was rather dimly lit. They managed to land on the drive at the entrance to the house by following the flickering candlelight coming from its windows. It had been built at the same time as Fetlocks Hall but was much smaller and squarer. It had a large conservatory to one side which was, in fact, Uncle Faustus's orangery.

Penny peered through the windows of the candle-lit dining room. Uncle Faustus was seated at the head of a long table, with his wife at the other end. Between them sat two children. The table was piled high with the most delicious-looking fruit and vegetables. A rather odd-looking tall, pale servant was serving their supper on silver plates.

Beneath the table lay several large grey dogs. Penny thought they were deerhounds just like Potty Smythe's until one stood up and yawned a toothy smile. To her horror she could see that it was a large rangy-looking wolf. Here and there, hanging from paintings, chandeliers and curtain rails were various bats. The servant disappeared and came back into the room with a large jug of what looked like . . . well . . . blood!

'Thank you, Eric,' said Uncle Faustus. 'Lovely and fresh. Squeezed it myself only this morning.'

Eric poured the red liquid into glass goblets for the family.

'Cheers,' said Uncle Faustus.

'*Santé*,' said his beautiful wife.

'Coffins up!' said the two children, and they all drank deeply from the goblets.

Patch shivered and took a step back from the window.

'Are you sure you want to go in there, Pen?' he asked hesitantly.

'They're supposed to be Veggipires and not vampires,' Penny replied. 'I'd probably taste awful to them.'

Leaving Patch by the railings she climbed the front steps and pulled the black iron handle of the bell pull by the side of the entrance. To her surprise it chimed the first few bars of the French national anthem.

She could hear slow, deliberate footsteps advancing from the other side of the door. Eric opened it and stared down at her in a rather sullen way with his mouth open.

'Please be so good as to tell Sir Faustus that Her Royal Highness, Penny Simms, one hundredth Unicorn Princess, is here to see him,' said Penny, pulling herself up to her full height and trying to sound important.

Eric nodded silently and showed her into a reception room. He motioned for her to take a seat and backed out of the room, closing the double doors behind him.

The room was not decorated in the style of a vampire's castle but looked like a French château. The windows were hung with beautiful white brocade curtains and golden tassels. The walls were covered with silk wallpaper in pale pink and silver stripes. Urns of fruit and flowers stood on tables, windowsills and the elaborate mantelpiece, above which hung a gold-framed mirror adorned with fauns and cherubs. Penny stood on her tiptoes to look in the mirror. In its reflection she saw a door opening and shutting behind her but she could not see anyone entering the room.

'Err, hum!' came a little cough and she turned to see a very handsome, tall, dark-haired man dressed in a black tailcoat and a white bow tie standing in the room. She looked again at the mirror but could not see him in it.

'How very odd,' she thought.

'Oh, I don't have a reflection, Your Highness,' said Uncle Faustus shyly, sweeping a lock of thick black hair behind one ear. He had deep, dark eyes, pale skin and very red lips for a man. 'To what do I owe the honour of your visit?' he asked, giving a polite bow.

Penny realised he knew exactly who and what she was in spite of her school uniform. He walked over, took her offered hand and gave it a kiss. Penny sat down on a gold chair and Faustus pulled a little black and silver case from his pocket. He opened it and offered her a small stick of celery!

'Thanks,' said Penny, choosing one and biting off a chunk.

'Sir Faustus,' she began, 'I have come here as the ambassador of King Valentine Silverwings, King of the Unicorns.'

'Oh yes,' said Uncle Faustus. 'I know who you are, of course. My relatives . . . well, you know . . . you're virtually part of my family.'

This made Penny feel much more comfortable.

'I'm sorry to interrupt your supper,' she continued, 'but they said this was the best time to come. There's a huge problem threatening the S.U.S. and Fetlocks Hall and we were all hoping you might be able to help.'

She told him about the Devliped curse and the rotten letter Despot Dragontail had sent to OGRIBS. Uncle Faustus sat down in a chair and gently nibbled on his piece of celery.

'Have you seen those smelly pony vampire bats in the mausoleum?' Penny asked.

'Oh yes,' he replied. 'Lovely specimens. Very rare.'

Penny was appalled at his reaction.

'They're horribly dangerous,' she gasped. 'When they wake up they'll bite all our ponies and turn them into pony vampires. They'll fly around Fetlocks pooing all over the place and stinking out the Health and Safety inspectors with their horrible breath when they visit. They haven't just been sent to ruin Fetlocks Hall by getting it closed down for being unhygienic, but to bite us all and turn us into vampires so that we cannot protect the Unicorns and the Equilibrium of Goodness!'

Uncle Faustus looked at the long black shiny toes of his shoes.

'I can't help that,' he said.

'Uncle Faustus,' said Penny sternly, 'if the Health and Safety inspectors discover you and your family they may just get the wrong idea. Dangerous wolves, bats, goblets of what looks like blood? You have your own children and wife to protect as much as I have Equilaw and Fetlocks Hall!'

At this Uncle Faustus stood up, walked over to the window and looked out into the night. Penny had to confess she was a little worried about his reaction to her outburst. For a moment she wished she had brought her Lance of Courage that defended her against all evil.

Uncle Faustus turned and stared at the little girl with his big dark eyes.

'Although I have no wish to see the Devlipeds succeed I owe nothing to Fetlocks Hall because the Fitznicelys have ignored me for hundreds of years. They have never accepted my wife, which has been deeply hurtful, and my children are scorned by their cousins. I wanted my son and daughter to be educated at Fetlocks but my half-brother and his wife would not hear of it. If you can persuade him to accept us for the harmless decent Veggipires we are I will do my best to help you.'

Penny couldn't believe her luck. She wanted to rush over and give him a hug but wasn't too sure about that, so she remained calm and princess-like safely in her chair.

'Thank you so much, Uncle Faustus,' she smiled. 'I'm sure they will if it means protecting their home, the school and the S.U.S. It's your chance to prove what nice people you are and that you have nothing to be ashamed of, but please help me to get rid of the pony vampires quickly. Who knows what they'll do when they wake up.'

Uncle Faustus beamed a handsome smile. Penny could see a little sharp tooth on either side of it.

'OK, Princess Penny,' he said. 'I'm on the case.

Would you like to meet my family and have a goblet of Fangley Zest?'

Penny said she would be delighted but would pass on the Zest. She didn't want to risk turning into a Veggipire by drinking it.

Uncle Faustus showed her into the dining room and introduced his beautiful French wife. Countess Mortia-Antoinette looked splendid in a vermilion cocktail dress, with her pearl necklace and earrings. Her black ringlets were perfectly pinned back with a red rose.

'These are my children,' said Uncle Faustus, 'the honourable – or dishonourable – Morriati and Mercedes.'

'We've heard all about you,' said Morri as the two of them came bounding up. Merc was dressed in a pretty white party dress with a red satin sash. Morri was wearing a smart black suit. 'We know about your bravery, your Equabatics and your cleverness, not from our snobby cousins up at the Hall but from Aunt Portia, who sneaks down here every so often to bring us bones for our wolves. We must go for a flight one night. We're all quite batty here at the Dower House, aren't we, Merc?'

Merc nodded, grinning a toothy grin exactly like her father's.

The wolves did not stir. They stayed under the table with their hackles up, following Penny with their yellow eyes.

'Come on, Luchie and Lobelia,' cooed the Countess. 'This is Princess Penny, she is very nice . . . No nipping now.' Suddenly feeling vulnerable, Penny wished she had brought Queen Starlight's Horn with her as it calmed wild beasts and hounds. But she had no need to worry. One by one the five wolves – Luchie, Lobelia, Lupin, Lavender and Phoenix – crept out from beneath the table.

'Sit,' said Countess Mortia and they all sat obediently.

'High five!' said Morri and they all held up a paw with deadly-looking claws.

'Down,' added Merc, 'and roll over.'

The wolves obeyed.

'You can tickle their tummies now,' she added. 'They love that.'

Penny summoned up all her courage and tickled Luchie's belly. He wiggled one of his back legs in appreciation and grinned. Penny repeated the treatment on the rest of his family, who instantly loved her. They were as soppy as Potty Smythe's deerhounds.

Countess Mortia asked Penny if she would like to

join them for pudding. Penny could not see any harm in it as long as she stayed clear of any blood oranges.

Morri politely pulled out a chair for her and held it while she seated herself at the table. Eric appeared with the most lovely peach and strawberry ice-cream sundae Penny had ever seen. She was beginning to like the Fangley-Fitznicelys.

The pretty French clock on the mantelpiece chimed twelve.

'It's been lovely meeting you all,' said Penny graciously, 'but it's time I was getting back to Fetlocks.'

'It's flying time for us,' said Morri and Merc. 'We'll come back with you.'

Uncle Faustus and Countess Mortia walked Penny out to the drive, where Patch was eating the rose bushes that were growing in a large urn.

'I'll be in touch as soon as I've worked something out,' said Faustus.

'The sooner the better,' said Penny, hopping up on Patch. 'Potty Smythe says OGRIBS could come at any moment.'

'Here's your escort party, Your Highness,' said the tall dark man, pointing up at the moon.

Two little bats were flitting about in its blue glow. It was Morri and Merc!

'Come on,' they shouted. 'Race you back to the Hall. Last one's a dead duck!'

'You're on,' shouted Penny. 'Come on, Patch, *Let's Fly!*'

Patch lifted off the ground and zoomed into the night sky but he was no match for the Fangley children. They ran rings round him all the way home.

Penny landed Patch in the stable yard. The two little bats had beaten her and were hanging upside down in Patch's stable. They climbed down the wall, getting bigger and bigger as they descended, changing back into their Veggipire forms.

Patch snorted and looked terrified.

'It's OK,' said Penny, stroking his neck. 'It's only Merc and Morri, Arabella and Antonia's cousins.'

'This is such a grand place!' said Merc. 'We are banned from it, of course, but they can't see us when we are bats so we fly over sometimes at night for a look round. We'd love to go to a school like this instead of having our tutor, old professor Spook, every day.'

Penny felt sorry for her two new friends. They were nice children and did not deserve to be excluded from Fetlocks just because they were Veggipires. She'd given her word that she'd speak to Sir Walter and Lady Sarah about their estranged relatives. She was confident that everything would be resolved because the Fitznicelys needed Uncle Faustus's help. Surely they would accept the family in return for his goodwill. If they took time to get to know them better they would realise what nice Veggipires they were.

Penny asked if Merc and Morri would like a tour of the yard. There were no two-legged inhabitants around at this time of night so no one would see them.

Merc and Morri were delighted to meet all the ponies, most of whom were lying down snoring.

She showed them the tack room with its cabinet of trophies and walls festooned with rosettes won from many shows and events over the years including the enormous silver Prince Phillip Cup Penny's team had won at the Horse of the Year Show.

Morri noticed Carlos's polo equipment stacked up in a corner.

Penny explained that they were forming a new Fetlocks Hall Flyers polo team.

'Ooooh,' he said. 'We'd love to play polo. It's something Merc and I have always dreamed of.'

'Can you ride?' asked Penny.

'*Can we ride?*' chipped in Merc. 'We've got our own ponies back at the Dower House. We can't fly them like you, but Nightsafe and Moonwalk are really fast and nippy. They'd make excellent polo ponies if you'd have us on your team.'

Penny thought this was a great idea. The team needed two more players with fast ponies. She told them she would ask Carlos because he was in charge of the team.

After their tour Merc and Morri gave Penny a hug and climbed up the wall of the clock tower, slowly changing back into their bat forms as they ascended. They wheeled round over Penny's head before darting across the moon back towards the Dower House.

Penny went to see if Patch was comfortable. He was fast asleep in his bed of golden straw, snoring his head off.

She walked back to the girls' dormitory she shared with Sam and Pip, thinking about the letter she had received from her older sister, Charlotte. It was all about the new vampire book she was reading. Penny smiled to herself. Whatever would her family think if they knew what had happened that night and that she had four new *real* Veggipire friends?

She'd have some careful diplomatic work to do on the Fitznicelys about her new chums at the Dower House. Also, she'd have to let the other Fetlocks Hall Flyers in on the consequences of the OGRIBS inspection because she was going to need their help. She yawned as she climbed the big wooden flight of stairs to her room.

That could wait until morning.

CHAPTER FOUR

Polo and Politics

At six in the morning Penny was back on the yard with her friends. The Flyers were talking about their exciting new polo club. Penny explained that she had met two nice children with fast ponies who would like to join.

'It would work really well,' she explained. 'They are brother and sister so we could have two teams: a girls' team and a boys' team of four players each.'

Carlos thought this was a brilliant idea.

'We'll give you a run for your money,' laughed Sam. Pip and Penny agreed with her.

Carlos asked Penny if she could bring her friends over on Sunday to knock the ball about.

Once the ponies were fed the children made their way back to the Hall for breakfast. As Penny walked up the aisle between the rows of tables in the refectory the Fitznicelys waved at her from their portraits in the usual way. Of course no one else ever saw this except Potty Smythe. Penny smiled up at them but could not wave back because that was secret S.U.S. business. The rest of the children would have thought she'd gone mad if they saw her waving at a wall. She did, however, walk past with both thumbs up behind her back which was the secret sign to say she needed to talk to the Fitznicelys later.

Morning assembly took place after breakfast and the headmistress briefed the other teachers about a staff meeting in H.Q. at lunchtime. She also informed the children that inspectors were due at the school shortly. She told them there was nothing to worry about and she was confident that they would answer all Swottworm's questions correctly because they were very clever, plucky fighters and had excellent teachers. She said she would let them know the inspection date later.

However, Septimus Swottworm had no intention of telling the school when he was coming. He was planning a surprise visit. He was going to test each class and its teachers, and try to catch the children out with difficult questions on their subjects.

When Potty Smythe returned to H.Q. she found an email waiting for her from the Health and Safety Department of OGRIBS.

Dr Meena Sweepover PhD and her assistant Mr Nigel Snoop from Health and Safety had given a date. They were planning to visit on the second of June. As it was now the twenty-ninth of May that meant in four days' time!

Things were really urgent now. The headmistress thought she'd better get Penny to visit the Dower House again to chase up Uncle Faustus. He didn't have long to come up with a way of getting rid of the pony vampires before the inspectors arrived and Penny didn't have much time to smooth things out between the two families as she had promised to do in return for his cooperation.

At lunchtime H.Q. was full of very worried teachers and other members of staff.

Potty Smythe explained that the Health and Safety inspectors would be arriving in four days' time and they should prepare for the worst. She still had no idea of the date of Swottworm's visit to test the children's school work.

'You can count on me,' said Henry Digit, head of Maths. 'My class is more than up to scratch and ready to cope with any questions Swottworm chucks at them, but if he asks ones in advance of their curriculum to catch us out . . . well, it just won't add up.'

'What about my kitchen?' asked Mrs Honeybun, the school cook. 'It be as clean as a whistle but what if them Health and Safety inspectors object? It be essentially a country kitchen. When I plucks a pheasant there do be feathers all over the floor and all bits 'n' pieces from other game what Ben's shot in the park. Our eggs is all free range and they will have a bit of dirt on 'em, not like them ones from the supermarket.'

'And how many languages does this Swottworm speak?' asked Cara de Lascasas, head of the modern languages centre. 'Is he going to ask questions in Martian to catch us out?'

'Calm down, chaps,' said Potty Smythe, crossing her fingers in her pockets. 'This is what we are going to do. I aim to get some advance information about when Swottybits is turning up. It's all about preparation so you'll have to start your classes on a crash swot-up right now. As for Dr Sweepover and Nigel

Snoop, we'll just have to be sure they only see what we want them to see. I'll let you know when I've found out more.'

She made notes of the meeting and had the school secretary, Kitty Baggins, make photocopies of them and send one to each member of staff.

Henrietta Wellington-Green, head girl of the stable staff, was always prepared. The yard was as safe as possible and immaculately clean at all times. But the inspectors might not know about ponies, who could be unpredictable and excitable at times. Even a misplaced hoof on a child's plimsoll could cause a broken toe.

'They'll probably be allergic to ponies anyway and sneeze their heads off,' chuckled Peter Fixcannon, the vet, as he prepared an injection of painkillers and muscle relaxants for a pony with colic. 'Just call their bluff, Henry. Put buckets of disinfectant everywhere for them to dip their city shoes in. Mustn't spread infection, you know . . . Health and Safety rules on a yard like this!'

'How clever of you,' beamed Henry, who had the most awful crush on the handsome vet.

Penny was sitting in the tack room on an upturned bucket studying the minutes of the staff meeting that Henry had left on the saddle horse.

She thought Potty's crash swot-up idea was great and wondered how she could help motivate the rest of the students to go for it. It certainly would help if they had some information about the time of the Swottworm visit and an idea of what kind of tricky questions he was likely to ask.

'Crikey!' she exclaimed when she read that the Health and Safety inspectors were coming in four days' time. 'Faustus had better get a move on and I'd better have a chat with the Fitznicelys.'

Just then Arabella and Antonia floated through the wall.

'We saw the thumbs-up sign, Penny,' said Arabella. 'What's the news? Have you found out what part our unspeakable relatives at the Dower House are playing in all this?'

Penny told them of her meeting with Uncle Faustus and his promise to help. She assured them that he had nothing to do with the pony vampires and the Devliped plot.

'They're a really nice family,' she said. 'Your cousins, Merc and Morri, are great fun. They ride really well and can fly better than I can. Why have you guys disowned them?'

'They're bats!' shrieked Arabella.

'Vile!' cried Antonia.

'That *Countess* mother of theirs is an imposter,' Arabella continued. 'She came from a peasant family of sheep herders in France. She says she's a Belle Fontaine indeed! It's more like Belle Mouton! She made the title up because she wanted to trap Uncle Faustus into marriage for wealth and position. She's nothing but a gold-digger and our family will never accept her because of it. Anyway, you can't have bats batting for Fetlocks Hall!'

'They're lovely fruit-eating bats,' said Penny. 'They don't hurt anybody. Merc says she and Morri have two really good ponies and dream of playing polo. They want to join our team.'

The twins were actually quite curious about their cousins but had never met them because their parents forbade it.

'Carlos says they can come over on Sunday for a practice,' said Penny. 'Why don't you join us and watch?'

The twins liked the idea. They were sure their parents would have no objection to them watching the new Fetlocks polo team practising.

'I can't say how important it is that your two families stop this silly feud,' Penny insisted. 'We really do need Uncle Faustus's help to get rid of the pony vampires. He's agreed to try if I can get your side of the family to accept the Fangleys.'

'Oh,' said the twins, looking at each other and making faces.

'We'll have to convince Papa and Mama but that's not going to be easy. Mama has a fit of the flutters every time the *Countess*'s name is mentioned,' said Antonia.

'To change the subject,' said Penny, 'I need you two to keep an eye out for that wretched Swottworm inspector. He could turn up unannounced at any moment as we don't exactly know when he's coming. The whole school is on a swot-up because we're not sure what sort of questions he's likely to ask.'

The twins looked at each other and smiled.

'I bet we can find out,' they said.

'Do you know Ethelene Giggabit, top of her class in Computer Studies?'

Penny did know Ethelene. She had a pony called Mouse.

'I bet she could hack into the OGRIBS computer and find out everything we need to know,' said Antonia.

Penny's eyes lit up. They were right. If anyone could get any information it was Ethelene, or Gig as she was known to her friends. She was a skinny, geeky little girl with a short pony tail like a docked horse and thick black spectacles. Mack Modem, head of Computer Studies, thought she was the bee's knees and would probably end up working for the government as a secret agent.

Penny and the twins made their way to the computer room, where they found Gig de-bugging one of the school machines.

'Hi, Penny,' she said, addressing the only one of the three of them she could see. 'Won't be a sec. This little chap's got worms – digital word worm to be exact . . . There, that's fixed it. Now, what can I do for you?'

Penny liked Gig – she was always helpful and efficient. Whenever the school needed new tack for the ponies Gig found the best deals on the Internet for them. Penny explained about the OGRIBS inspection and asked if Gig could somehow find out when Swottworm was arriving so that everyone could be prepared.

Gig said she would have a go but it might take an hour or so.

'I hope she finds out quickly,' said Antonia.

'I'll keep you posted,' said Penny, hurrying away to her last lesson of the day, English Literature, with Miss Belinda Penn.

The subject the teacher had chosen for today was 'The History of the Vampire in Literature from 1800 to the Present Day'. Penny wondered if anyone had written anything about pony vampires before as she might learn something useful. In fact, after an hour with Miss Penn, it became quite clear that 'The Unwelcome Intrusion' of Fetlocks Hall was a first in vampire history!

After class Penny rushed back to the Computer Studies department to find Gig hard at work.

'I wish this was as easy as hacking out with Mouse,' she said as Penny walked in. 'But . . . yes, here it is.'

A stream of paper came out of the printer, which she gathered up and put into a blue plastic folder for Penny, together with a disk containing all the information on it. She labelled it 'Top Secret Swottworm Alert'!

Penny glanced at the top page. Her mouth fell open.

SWOTTWORM INVASION SCHEDULED FOR JUNE 1ST.

That was in three days' time. The day before the Health and Safety inspection!

Gig had done more than expected. She had searched the Internet to find the most likely questions ever asked by examiners on each school subject.

There was an impressive list of questions and answers and a list of the most likely Health and Safety features Dr Sweepover and Mr Snoop might check at Fetlocks!

'Thanks, Gig,' said Penny. 'You are a Digital Diva. You just saved our bacon.'

She tucked the folder under her arm and ran for H.Q.

'My goodness!' said Potty Smythe as she read the file. 'How did you get hold of this, young lady?'

Penny told her it was all thanks to Ethelene Giggabit.

The headmistress sent an email to all members of staff inviting them to another extraordinary meeting in which she intended to brief them on the questions. They would help the students with the serious swotting they had to do in the next few days.

She was a bit concerned about the Health and Safety inspection programme.

They wanted to check everything including the swimming pool and the school grounds. The pool had not been used for years and was very green and slimy. Old Mr Pennypot, the gardener and groundsman, had been breeding leeches in it and selling them to the local hospital.

As for the grounds themselves, she hoped the inspectors would not get as far as the mausoleum and the Dower House.

CHAPTER FIVE

The Night Match

Potty Smythe asked Penny if she'd check up on the progress Uncle Faustus was making, so Penny thought she'd better go and see him as soon as it was dark and warn him of the short amount of time before the Health and Safety inspection. She hoped he had already found a way of persuading the pony vampires to go home.

She flew Patch over and left him talking to Moonwalk and Nightsafe in the home paddock

53

to the Dower House. The five Fangley-Fitznicely wolves came rushing out to greet her, rolling over to have their tummies tickled. Phoenix, the youngest of them, grabbed her sock with his teeth. It was very hard to walk with a playful wolf holding on to her footwear.

She noticed that Lupin was looking very plump and wondered if she'd eaten something big like a sheep.

'She's pregnant,' said a delighted Uncle Faustus, climbing down a nearby wall as he changed from a bat into his usual shape. 'Lots of little puppies to come. Would you like one, Penny?'

Penny would have loved a wolf puppy but said she was worried about how the deerhounds and terriers would react up at the Hall.

'No problem,' smiled Uncle Faustus. 'They come over regularly to play with each other. I'm sure Aunt Portia will let you have one.'

Penny was overjoyed but wondered what her parents would say when she came home for the holidays with a wolf. What would the neighbours in Milton Keynes say to one roaming around in the garden? She changed the subject to more important things and asked Uncle Faustus if he had any news on the pony vampires.

'I've just come back from the mausoleum,' he said shyly, 'and, well . . . they've gone.'

Penny gave a huge sigh of relief.

'Oh, you are clever,' she said, beaming. 'I suppose they've gone back home to Transylvania.'

'Well, not exactly,' said Uncle Faustus, pointing a long finger up at the sky.

To Penny's horror, whirling around the chimney-pots of the Dower House were dozens of large black shapes. A large plop of orange pony vampire poo landed on her foot and her heart sank.

She was beginning to agree with Arabella and Antonia that Uncle Faustus could be completely useless.

'They've just woken up,' he whispered. 'They'll be hungry now. I put out some Fangley Zest for them in little bowls but they won't touch it. I'm working on it though. I have an idea for a new recipe.'

Penny was losing her patience with Faustus.

'There are only four days left before the inspectors arrive!' she said.

Uncle Faustus seemed completely unperturbed about the inspectors. He was more worried about the pony vampires. He told her that they would sleep during the day as long as they could get back into the mausoleum and nobody sealed up their secret entrance. 'But I'm afraid unless I can convert them to

Veggipiredom by finding something they'd like to eat rather than blood they will start feeding tonight and every night from now on.'

Penny had no option but to put her trust in him. But the most important thing now was to get back to Fetlocks as soon as possible and tell Potty Smythe the bad news. They'd have to lock up all the ponies at night and hang strings of garlic round their necks.

She ran back to the Dower House paddock to fetch Patch. He was standing by the gate looking worried, with Moonwalk and Nightsafe fastidiously licking his neck.

'I didn't see it coming!' he said in Equalese. Penny lifted up his long brown and white mane. On the near side by the jugular groove of his neck were two little red holes.

'A pony vampire has bitten him,' said Moonwalk. 'There's nothing we can do except lick the wound to prevent infection!'

'Oh, Patch,' cried Penny, bursting into tears. 'Is he going to die?'

'No,' said Nightsafe, 'he will never do that but he'll sprout wings and become one of them before the sun gets up. He will fly away with the flock and won't be your friend any more!'

Penny sobbed into Patch's mane.

'I feel a bit weak, Pen,' he said, sinking to his knees.

There was no time to lose. Penny had to pull herself together and act instantly.

'Nightsafe,' she said, stifling her tears, 'stay with him and make sure they don't come back for another bite. Moonwalk and I will fly over to Fetlocks to fetch something to help Patch.'

'And how do I keep them off?' asked Nightsafe, looking up at the moonlit sky whirling with pony vampires. 'They'll probably bite me as well!'

Penny thought quickly. She remembered Miss Penn's lesson and the list of things vampires hated like fire, garlic, sunlight and crosses, but she had none of these things to protect Patch and Nightsafe. She glanced up at the swirling black shapes over the treetops. Silhouetted against the bright moon, two branches of a tree were making a cross.

Penny had a brilliant idea.

'Come on, Moonwalk,' she said, climbing on to his back. '*Let's Fly!*' The little black pony lifted off the ground and Penny steered him towards the branches. Luckily they were old dry wood so it was easy for her to break two pieces off. He hovered in mid-air while she detached them from the oak tree.

'Down,' she said and he gently landed by Patch. Penny slid off and quickly pulled some of Patch's tail hair out to bind the branches together in the shape of a cross. Nightsafe dug a hole in the soil with her foot and Penny planted the cross in it near Patch, who was now completely unconscious.

She told Nightsafe to stay by it for protection until she and her brother returned.

With that she jumped back on to Moonwalk. 'Come on, boy – *Let's Fly!*' she said. 'We have to go like lightning!' She hung on to his black mane as he sped up into the sky and jetted towards Fetlocks Hall. Merc and Morri were right. Their ponies were dead nippy.

As soon as they landed by the front entrance to Fetlocks, Penny dismounted and charged up to the fifth step, where she kept her magical gifts. The stone unicorns shot out the usual rainbow of stars from their eyes as the step sprang open to reveal the gifts all laid out on a golden cushion. The precious vial of Unicorn Tears used to cure all wounds and illnesses jumped into Penny's hand, followed by the Lance of Courage. In a flash she was back on Moonwalk and streaming away through the night sky towards the Dower House paddock, where poor Patch lay motionless on the grass with a very frightened Nightsafe by his side, cowering behind the cross. Above them, whirling and screaming, were dozens of hungry pony vampires. Moonwalk suddenly came to a stop in mid-air.

'Crikey!' he said. 'I'm not flying through that lot.'

'Trust me,' said Penny, 'I am a Unicorn Princess and I can do anything. We have to get through those creatures and save your sister and Patch. I'm not sure how long my makeshift cross will work. It hasn't been blessed and I think they suspect it's a fake!'

Moonwalk gritted his teeth. 'OK,' he said, 'I won't let you down, but I will *get* you there.'

Penny pulled the Lance of Courage out of her waistband and pointed it at the pony vampires. The little silver cane grew into a magnificent and terrifying lance. It glowed blue and flashes of lightning shot out from its spear head.

'*Let's Fly!*' she screamed.

'Let's charge!' shouted Moonwalk, laying back his black ears as they shot through the dark shapes. Penny wielded the lance like a polo stick, batting the pony vampires out of the way and clearing a path in the air for Moonwalk to fly in.

She remembered the polo strokes Carlos had taught her.

The offside forehand . . . WHACK . . . She caught one of the beasts on the head and it flopped to the ground.

The offside neck shot . . . SWISH . . . She expertly leaned under Moonwalk's neck and dealt another one a blow.

The nearside neck shot . . . SPLAT . . . She sent a pony vampire squealing into a spin of flapping wings.

The offside tail shot . . . CRACK . . . She whacked one on the nose as it tried to attack from behind.

The nearside back hand . . . POW . . . Another flipped over the treetops.

The nearside back shot . . . THWACK . . . This difficult shot, when mastered, is the second most powerful. She sent a row of the pony vampires flying, their furry bodies colliding like a stack of playing cards.

'You are amazing!' gasped Moonwalk, darting between his oncoming opponents like a high-goal polo pony.

'You're not bad yourself!' grinned Penny.

'You wait till you see Merc and Nightsafe in action,' Moonwalk went on. 'They do it all side-saddle.'

Penny couldn't even think how this would be possible but she had other things on her mind. They were over Patch and Nightsafe now. Somehow the makeshift cross had held out and the pony vampires had flown away. She settled Moonwalk down beside Patch. Nightsafe was sweating, her black coat glistening in the moonlight.

'I think he's . . . gone,' she cried, nuzzling Patch's motionless body.

Penny slid off Nightsafe's brother and took the vial of Unicorn Tears out of her pocket. She flipped open the lid and trickled a tiny drop of silver magic liquid on to each of the little red marks on Patch's neck. They instantly disappeared, but Patch remained frozen. Penny bit her lip. Maybe Unicorn Tears didn't work on vampire bites. Then suddenly, to her relief, Patch gave a snort and opened his eyes.

'I bet I missed a pretty good fight,' he said.

'Penny and Moonwalk were incredible,' said Nightsafe, licking his ear. 'You are the luckiest pony in the world to have a friend like Penny.'

'And I'm the luckiest girl in the world to have you, Patch,' grinned Penny, throwing her arms round his neck.

The little skewbald pony stood up and shook himself.

Penny thanked Nightsafe and Moonwalk for being so brave. Patch was completely cured now and able to fly home. The sun was just coming up over the mausoleum. The pony vampires should have returned and be safely asleep inside. Penny thought she would just drop in to make sure so she landed Patch outside and climbed up the steps. She fumbled for the key behind the gargoyle but it was not there. Gently she pushed the wooden door, which slowly creaked open. Surprisingly, the oil lamp and the matches were also missing. Someone must be in the crypt.

Penny fumbled her way down the dark stone staircase. There was a light coming from underneath a small low door to the side of the main chamber containing the tombs. Penny looked up and thought she could make out the shape of the sleeping pony vampires in the rafters above. A cold shiver ran down her spine as she gently turned the door handle.

'Come in, Princess Penny,' said a familiar voice.

Uncle Faustus did not look up. He was studying an ancient-looking book.

'Time is running out,' he said. 'Since the Fangley Zest didn't work on the pony vampires I am searching for a reference to anything else that might persuade them to go home.'

Penny looked around. She seemed to be in a small library with shelves of dusty books lining the walls.

'Oh yes,' continued Uncle Faustus, still with his nose in the book. 'The mausoleum has a library. It can be difficult to get to sleep if you are undead. A good book always sends us off. You can help me, Penny. Have a look and see if you can find anything to do with pony vampires.'

'I'll try,' said Penny, walking over to the shelves.

There were all sorts of old books with strange titles like *Werewolves: Husbandry and Restraint* by Dr Hyde and *Bat Keeping for Beginners* by Sir Faustus Fangley-Fitznicely.

'I didn't know you were an author,' said Penny, removing the book from the shelf and taking a closer look. When she tried to return it to its place, something seemed to prevent it from slotting back between the others. She took it out again and felt inside the space. Her fingers touched another book hidden behind . . . Pulling it out, she wiped the dust off the black leather cover to reveal a faded gold embossed title:

The History of the Pony Vampire by Count Derek Racula.

Remembering her Vampires in English Literature lesson with Miss Penn, Penny thought the name on the cover seemed quite familiar.

She opened a page marked with a red leather bookmark.

There in front of her very eyes was a little story about how Count Derek (obviously a proper vampire) had been blamed by the local Transylvanian peasants for killing their goats. In fact it was a flock of hungry pony vampires that were sucking them dry. The villagers threatened to burn down his castle, so the clever Count invented a special pony mix for the pony vampires to eat. It was a complete success. In fact they preferred it to blood and became Veggipire ponies. Slowly he added more and more grass to the mix until they were happy to graze peacefully on the Transylvanian mountainsides.

The Count had even listed details of the special mix:

1) *Crush as many old dry bones and dried blood oranges as possible to a fine powder.*
2) *Add salt, pepper and a teaspoon of cod liver oil.*
3) *Add grass cuttings gradually to the mixture, starting with a cupful for the first night feed.*
4) *Gradually decrease the mix and increase the grass content of the feed over three weeks. At the end of this time they will become complete herbivores and happy to eat only grass.*

Penny could not believe her luck. Surely this was exactly what they were looking for!

The old red leather bookmark fell on to the flagstone floor. When she picked it up she noticed an interesting inscription on one side. It read: *The Secret Life of Louis IV, King of France.*

It must have been an old bookmark belonging to that particular volume.

When she turned it over, it showed an engraving of the family tree of the King and his girlfriend, Madame de Montespan. Penny followed the branches of the tree down to their great-granddaughter Countess Magdelenne. According to the family tree she married one Count Belle Fontaine. They had a daughter called Mortia-Antoinette Belle Fontaine. If this was a true document it was quite clear that Uncle Faustus's wife was the great-great-granddaughter of Louis IV and a real countess after all!

Penny showed Uncle Faustus her two extraordinary finds.

His big dark eyes glowed as he read the pony mix recipe and sparkled with tears when he saw the family tree on the bookmark.

'I knew it was true,' he said, giving Penny a big hug, 'and now I know why you are a Unicorn Princess, Penny. You are the most amazing little girl! Come on, let's go home. Leave everything to me.' He took her hand and they made their way up the dark stairs and out into the early morning mist, where Patch was waiting to take Penny back to Fetlocks Hall.

Penny was relieved that everyone was safe for the rest of the day. But something had to be done by nightfall or many more ponies like poor Patch would get bitten. She could only treat one at a time with

Unicorn Tears. If lots were attacked at once by the pony vampires they might be converted before she could get to them. She could try her best to protect the Fetlocks ponies by locking them up in their stables with garlic round their necks but she would be unable to save all the other ponies in the area.

Now she had found the solution to the problem it was up to Uncle Faustus to work all day to make the right mixture.

Penny and Patch were exhausted. It was really hard work to fly back to the Hall without falling asleep that morning, but Penny had to tell Potty Smythe the good news about the recipe and show the Fitznicelys the little leather bookmark she was carrying in her blazer pocket.

CHAPTER SIX

Boning Up

The morning sun burst through the tall windows of H.Q. on the upper floors of Fetlocks Hall. Potty Smythe was briefing the other teachers on the results of Ethelene Giggabit's research. She had to confess she still had not the faintest idea how she was going to steer the Health and Safety inspectors away from certain things they would probably want to see. For a start, they would be horrified at Mr Pennypot's leech farm in the school swimming pool. He simply refused to do anything about it because leeches are rare and the local hospital needed them badly. Then they would have a fit when they saw the school kitchen. Although Mrs Honeybun scrubbed it to perfection it was essentially a Georgian one. It would never be the stainless steel state-of-the-art culinary workplace recommended by OGRIBS.

The children's dormitories were very comfortable. Three children usually shared one large room full of sagging sofas, unmade beds, dogs, toys, old copies of *Horse and Hound* and *Pony* magazine, books, strewn clothes and bits of straw and wood shavings from the ponies' beds that had become lodged in socks and shoes. Matron, Mrs Dogberry, tried her best each day to clean everything up but as soon as it was tidy the children untidied it again.

'It's like painting the Forth Bridge,' she complained, shaking her duster at Potty Smythe. 'As soon as you finish at one end you have to start again at the other!'

To make matters worse Sydney Sidewinder, the school janitor, had tried to mend the school boiler only to have it blow up and take the boiler-house roof with it. Now there was no hot water in the school and everybody had to take cold showers. As an aftershock of the explosion the Georgian copper pipes burst in Potty Smythe's bathroom and lifted her bath high into the air on a jet of bright blue water. Luckily she was not in it at the time but it landed with a crash and dislodged an enormous chandelier in the ceiling of the great hall below. Covered in hundreds of years of cobwebs and dust it crashed to the ground, shattering into a million tiny pieces as it hit the flagstone floor. This caused complete chaos because all the dogs had to be locked up until every scrap and splinter was vacuumed up in case the pieces of glass got stuck in their paws.

Mrs Dogberry burst into tears.

'Oh, do kick on, dear,' said Potty Smythe, putting a stout arm round her shoulders. 'It was much easier in the long run than having to get up there and clean it. The weight of the grime alone would have brought it down one day.'

Having left Patch snoring in his stable, a very tired Penny Simms stumbled into the great hall and crunched her way across the broken glass. She gave Potty Smythe the secret double thumbs-up sign so the headmistress gave Mrs Dogberry a paper hanky out of her pocket and walked Penny into the butler's pantry for a private chat.

'The pony vampires have woken up,' said Penny,

and she related last night's adventure. Potty Smythe congratulated her on her cleverness and bravery. She gave her the rest of the day off to visit Uncle Faustus and help him in any way she could.

Meanwhile the teachers had briefed their students on the questions Swottworm was most likely to ask them. They were all boning up on the possible answers ready for his visit.

They were not the only ones messing around with bones. The Fangley-Fitznicely wolves had raided the bone factory in Denge wood, on the other side of Longburton. It was a horribly smelly place where butchers' bones were delivered and ground up to make bone meal for fertiliser. Now there was a huge pile of them on the lawn outside the Dower House. Penny and Patch caught sight of it as they flew over later that morning.

Uncle Faustus was in the orangery tending the Fangley Zest. He was singing quietly to himself and wearing a large straw hat and dark sunglasses. He started as Penny came in through the glass doors.

'Oh, hello,' he said, watering a small sapling orange tree. He seemed very relaxed and unconcerned considering the crisis with the pony vampires.

Penny opened her mouth to speak but Uncle Faustus just held up his hand and told her to follow him. They picked their way across the bone-strewn lawn to a long dark shed. There was a strange crunching noise coming from it. He opened the double doors to reveal an ancient stone circular cider press with a huge granite wheel being pulled round by Moonwalk and Nightsafe. Merc, Morri and their mother were throwing bones and dried blood oranges into the round trough. The wheel was crushing them up into powder. Eric was mixing the powder with salt, pepper and cod liver oil and pouring it into buckets.

Penny was completely astounded by this joint family venture.

'Fangley Zest Blood Orange and Bone Pony Vampire Mix,' said Uncle Faustus proudly. 'I'm going to try it out on them at dusk.'

'What happens if they won't eat it?' asked Penny.

'Oh, they will,' he replied.

Penny just had to get back and tell Potty Smythe and the Fitznicelys.

She was sure Sir Walter and Lady Sarah would accept the Fangleys as part of their family once they knew what nice people they were and how they had worked so hard to get rid of the pony vampires. She also had written proof on the bookmark of Countess Mortia's noble birth.

Back at the Hall she twisted the wooden unicorn

on the first banister of the great staircase as this was the usual way of summoning the Fitznicely family, who floated down from their portraits to join her. Penny told them that she had found a solution to the pony vampire problem and Uncle Faustus was going to try it out at dusk at the mausoleum.

Penny suggested that they all go over there at twilight to watch the proceedings.

Lady Sarah said she could not possibly go if Faustus's wife was going. Sir Walter said he would have to support her decision and decline the invitation too.

Penny thought it was time to play her trump card so she pulled the bookmark out of her pocket and handed it to Sir Walter, who looked at the family tree and passed it to his wife.

'Oh, my goodness!' he laughed. 'What huge fun and what a wonderful scandal, my dear. Thanks to Penny we can dine out on this for years! What larks we will have telling the Montecutes and the de Parrotts that we have real royal French blood in the family!'

Lady Sarah was most amused.

'This changes everything,' she smiled. 'We would be delighted to come over this evening and congratulate my sister-in-law, the Countess Mortia-Antoinette Belle Fontaine, on her family tree!'

Arabella and Antonia giggled behind their hands and said they would look forward to meeting their noble cousins.

Lady Sarah was concerned for Penny, Patch and Aunt Portia. 'What happens if the pony vampires won't eat the mixture or prefer your blood to it? They can't hurt us,' she said. 'We're dead already and have no blood. We are completely unappetising to them.'

Penny said she would bring her Lance of Courage, the vial of Unicorn Tears and Queen Starlight's Horn just in case.

She felt exhausted and thought she might need her strength for later if things didn't go according to plan at the twilight meeting. Mrs Honeybun brought some ham salad sandwiches and a flask of tea up to her room, where she fell asleep.

At 8 p.m. she woke up with a start. Something was tickling her nose. It was Arabella's hand and it was completely detached from her body. The twins were sitting at the bottom of her bed, giggling.

'Er . . . Bella, I do wish you wouldn't do that,' said Penny. 'It really is disgusting.'

Bella grabbed her hand and stuck it back on to the end of her arm. Penny followed them down the stairs and out of the front entrance, where Potty Smythe was waiting, flanked by her two pet unicorns Hippolita and Rain. Lady Sarah and Sir Walter were already mounted on their horses. Two pale-looking grooms in eighteenth-century costume, who Penny had never seen before, were holding the twins' ponies.

While the grooms helped the Fitznicely girls to mount, Penny fetched her magical gifts from their hiding place and whistled to Patch, who came galloping across the park. She opened the field gate for him, jumped on his back and joined the others.

Potty Smythe said she'd drive over in the Land Rover.

The unicorns waved goodbye with their wings as the cavalcade set off for the woods and the mausoleum.

A similar procession was heading for the meeting place from the Dower House. Countess Mortia and Uncle Faustus were travelling in a fine black carriage drawn by two black horses and driven by Eric, flanked by Merc and Morri on their ponies. They were followed by a farm cart stacked with buckets of the Fangley Zest Blood Orange and Bone Pony Vampire Mix. It was drawn by a gentle dray horse driven by the one-eyed peasant who acted as groom at the Dower House.

Dusk was falling. Outside the mausoleum the two families greeted each other with smiles while Eric and the one-eyed peasant carried the buckets over to an overgrown hole at the back of the building. This was the pony vampires' secret entrance to the mausoleum.

The sun crept behind the trees in Duns Copse as the stable clock struck nine.

'Stand back, everybody,' said Uncle Faustus. 'They're waking up.'

Suddenly masses of large pony vampires flew out of the hole in the ground and flitted round the buckets in sweeping circles. Some just flew up above the trees and seemed completely uninterested. Penny was worried they might not like their new feed.

'What happens if they prefer us?' whispered Patch.

'It's OK,' replied Penny, her hand on the Lance of Courage tucked into the waistband of her school skirt.

Even Potty Smythe looked a bit apprehensive.

'I'm glad I'm dead,' said Arabella.

'Maybe I could throw my hand at them to distract the things if they attack,' said Antonia. 'It might divert their attention if they think it's alive.'

'Look,' said Uncle Faustus, pointing at one of the pony vampires, who seemed to be sniffing at a bucket. 'That one looks quite interested!'

It stuck its head in the bucket and started gobbling the stuff.

'He seems to be enjoying it,' said Lady Sarah, smiling at Countess Mortia.

'I hope so,' she replied graciously. 'It took us most of the day to prepare.'

The rest of the pony vampires obviously thought their friend was on to a good thing and flew in to take a closer sniff. They swirled down from the treetops, pounced on their gourmet meal of Fangley Mix and gobbled it all up greedily.

Full of food, they became very pleasant and tame. Several of them were lying on their backs, burping.

Uncle Faustus walked over to the biggest one and patted it on the head. It smiled a toothy grin and levitated itself just enough off the ground so that he could throw a leg over its back. Once he was seated he flew it around in a couple of circles to get the hang of it, then beckoned to the other pony vampires. They lazily flopped into the air and followed their leader carrying Uncle Faustus, his cloak billowing out behind him, into the dusk.

Merc, Morri and their mother waved him farewell.

'Where's your dad gone?' asked Penny.

'Oh, he'll be back soon,' said Merc.

'He's gone for a short holiday to Transylvania to visit some old chums,' added Morri.

'He's taking the pony Veggipires home,' said the Countess.

'Thank you so much for everything you've done,' said Lady Sarah. 'We are most grateful for your family's help in ridding our mausoleum of these horrible creatures.'

'We'd be honoured if you and the children would come to dinner at Fetlocks Hall one evening, wouldn't we, dear?' said Sir Walter, taking his wife's arm.

Countess Mortia gave a gracious nod and said she'd be pleased to accept.

Penny and Potty Smythe winked at each other. Penny gave a sigh of relief.

'Well *done*, Penny,' whispered the headmistress.

CHAPTER SEVEN

Team Spirits

Sunday arrived. Carlos had arranged for the practice polo match on the newly prepared polo ground, smartly marked out with the new boards and goalposts Matt's dad had sent. Set out in front of the Hall it looked very professional indeed.

The children were really excited and could not wait to get started. Back in the stable yard Carlos put out eight upturned milk crates in a row for his unmounted teams to stand on and practise their shots. Everyone had been given a sheet of paper with the rules of the game on it. They were all studying their copies when Merc and Morri rode in under the stable archway. Penny ran over to them and gave their ponies a hug.

'Hiya, Princess,' said Morri.

'We're up 'n' running,' said Merc.

She was riding Nightsafe side-saddle, wearing a modern black side-saddle apron, a black shirt and tie, a black velvet waistcoat with silver buttons, crash hat with a black velvet 'silk' (a covering with a peak) turned up in a very professional way and dark sunglasses. Morri was astride, of course, wearing black breeches, boots, knee pads, a black polo shirt, and the same style crash hat, silk and dark glasses as his sister. Sitting on their lovely black shiny ponies Penny thought they really looked the business.

The others stopped in their tracks and stared at the two strange-looking riders. Penny walked over with the Fangley children and introduced them to the rest of the team. Carlos had already told them that there would be two prospective team members trying for a place today. He was not quite prepared for Merc and Morri, but had to admit they looked pretty cool. They smiled toothy grins and asked when could they start.

Moonwalk and Nightsafe were put into stables next door to Patch while the children stood on the upturned crates and practised their shots under Carlos's instruction.

To Henry's delight Peter Fixcannon had volunteered to come over with his ex-race horse, Charlotte Allstar, and help Carlos demonstrate some tactics. He had played professional polo for the Hurtlington Polo Club when he was a student.

Peter swung into the lorry park with his car and trailer. Henry helped him unbox Charlotte. She thought he looked even more handsome as he rode out on to the ground in his red polo shirt, white breeches, brown boots, knee protectors, helmet and visor with his polo stick over his shoulder.

Once the children had read the rules and practised their shots they mounted up and followed Carlos and Budget out to join Peter.

They lined up on the outside of the ground to watch as Henry threw in the ball.

Carlos and Peter shook hands and started the demonstration with some offensive and defensive plays.

Peter hit the ball with an offside forehand and chased after it at full gallop with Carlos in pursuit. Just as he was about to strike it for the second time Carlos demonstrated 'Riding Off', in which he made

Budget push Charlotte away from the ball so that he could gain control of it. Budget knew exactly what to do, being an ex-high-goal pony, but poor Charlotte was a bit scared.

Carlos now had the ball so he gave it a powerful nearside forehand and whacked it between the goalposts.

Everyone cheered.

Henry threw the ball in again and Carlos took it, galloping up the ground with Budget expertly chasing it. Peter sped up and came alongside. When Carlos swung his mallet to hit the ball again Peter cleverly hooked it with his own mallet to restrict Carlos's shot. This defensive move, known as 'hooking', enabled him to take the ball. He sent it winging between the goalposts at the opposite end of the ground with an impressive offside neck shot.

They also demonstrated fouls for which the three umpires overseeing a match would give penalty points to the offending team. There was to be no 'Dangerous Horsemanship' – for example, a player must not cross his opponent's pony's back legs as it could cause a fall.

Budget had been very kind to Charlotte once she realised the poor thing had never played polo before. Whenever she was about to make an offensive move she shouted in Equalese to warn her she was coming. She also taught Charlotte how to defend herself from injury and chase the ball.

Peter Fixcannon had no idea this conversation was going on. He was most impressed with Charlotte's progress.

'You are the best girl in my life,' he told her as he scored another triumphant goal.

Penny, of course, could hear dear old Budget shouting instructions. She thought she would be the best teacher possible for all the other team ponies. Under her guidance they would be unbeatable!

Carlos and Peter explained polo talk like 'Take the man first', 'Tail it' and 'Turn it' – all phrases used by players asking for the ball to be passed to them.

By the end of the demonstration both ponies and their riders were soaking wet with sweat. Peter's red polo shirt was sticking to his back.

Henry came out of the Hall with a tray of jugs and glasses of home-made freshly squeezed ice cold lemonade which Mrs Honeybun had just prepared. Merc and Morri carried little silver flasks of Fangley Zest for their refreshment.

They all sat on the grass as Carlos explained how a team worked together.

'Team players are numbered 1, 2, 3 and 4,' he said.

'Number 1 is the attacking or offensive player. He concentrates on opportunities for scoring. The defensive player is Number 4. He defends the goal and tries to stop the opposing team players getting control of the ball. Number 3 player stems his opponent's attack and is in charge of passing the ball to Number 1 and Number 2 players. Number 2 player supports Number 3's job.'

After their break and a good deal of cold lemonade Carlos and Peter changed ponies to Shilling, Budget's daughter, and Ned Kelly, Henry's ex-racehorse. Budget and Charlotte were tired now so Ben Faloon, Henry's right-hand man on the yard, took them back to the stables and gave them a nice cold hosing-down.

The two expert players partnered the children one by one to demonstrate how to pass the ball to each other and score goals. Carlos had no idea how Merc was going to play polo side-saddle. Actually, he did not believe it was possible until she aggressively rode him off, hooked his mallet, took control of the ball, galloped like a demon down the ground and whacked it between the goalposts before he had time to catch her!

Penny heard a round of ghostly applause from the side of the polo ground. It was the Fitznicely family.

There they were all looking beautiful in the fashion of their day, picnicking on strawberries and cream. Sitting in a wicker armchair in their midst was Countess Mortia, looking very proud of her daughter.

Morri and Moonwalk sped past Peter, who had hit the ball to Dom. He intercepted it and scored another goal with an impressive nearside neck shot from mid-ground!

In fact the Fangley children were both so awesome Carlos made them Number 1 attacking players of both the girls' and the boys' teams.

Patch was still apprehensive about playing polo. He was plump with short legs and not the fastest pony in the world. But Penny coaxed him through the practice session, explaining the tactics to him all the time, swinging her mallet as well as she had done during her night match with the pony vampires. By the end of the afternoon Patch was enjoying the game as much as his friends.

Arabella and Antonia were dying to have a go at polo. When the practice was over they floated up to Merc and Morri and asked if they could come over to the Dower House for some lessons. Sir Walter and Lady Sarah told Countess Mortia how proud they were of their talented niece and nephew.

'And your girls ride side-saddle very well,' she

replied. 'They look most elegant in those lovely habits.'

Penny smiled to herself. The Fangley Zest Blood Orange and Bone Pony Vampire Mix had worked in more ways than one. Not only had it converted the horrid things to peaceful Veggipiredom, it had united the two families.

Of course only Potty Smythe and Penny could see any of this. The headmistress gave the little girl a wink and held a finger up to her lips, the usual S.U.S. sign for saying 'This is our secret'.

'We'll have to be equally on the ball tomorrow, Penny,' she said as they all walked back to the stable yard. 'Swottworm is invading us at 9 a.m.!'

CHAPTER EIGHT

Dr Swottworm
Turns the Screw

'He's coming, he's coming!' shouted Arabella and Antonia, appearing though the wall in H.Q. They'd been sitting on the rusty iron gates at the end of the drive waiting for Swottworm's arrival.

Potty Smythe looked out of the window to see a small green bug-like car creeping up the carriage drive to the front steps. She told the twins to appear to Penny quickly so that she could alert the teachers and other students.

'I'll stall him,' she said, rushing down the stairs.

Septimus Swottworm was a small weedy man in a grey suit. He had thinning lank greasy hair swept over his bald crown and wore thick plastic glasses stuck on his pimply nose. He got out of his car carrying a brief-case, tape recorder and camera.

As he made his way up the steps his spectacles were suddenly plastered with a sticky silvery liquid. One of the stone unicorns had spat at him.

Potty Smythe, waiting at the entrance to the Hall, stifled a giggle and handed him a paper handkerchief from her pocket.

'It's the house martins,' she smiled. 'They get everywhere at this time of the year.'

Swottworm snatched the tissue from her hand and wiped his glasses.

'Let's get on with it, then,' he snarled, passing the headmistress his identity card and a list of subjects he wanted to inspect.

Potty Smythe led him along the corridors, stopping to point out important photographs of school achieve-ments and pictures of famous past pupils at Fetlocks.

'Oh, come on, woman,' he snarled. 'I haven't got all day.'

'We'll start with the Maths class as it's first on your list,' she said, opening a classroom door. 'Professor Henry Digit in attendance.'

The children stood up politely as Swottworm slouched in and Henry Digit came over, offering his hand in welcome. The creep completely ignored it and poked around the classroom, looking at the students' exercise books and testing the length of rulers.

Then he pounced on the children, asking them awkward questions like 'What is the square root of pi?' and 'What is the sum of the angles of an isosceles triangle?'

Of course the students had swotted up on the subject and answered all the questions confidently and correctly.

Swottworm scowled and moved on to Miss Chronicle's History class. He questioned the children in the same way and again received correct answers.

In fact all the students' work, in every class he visited, was of a very high standard.

Swottworm was fuming.

At the end of his tour Potty Smythe asked him up to her study for a cup of tea.

At his request she poured him half a weak cup which he sipped with his little thin wrinkly lips. They reminded her of a chicken's bottom.

She asked him if he was pleased with the results of his inspection.

'I'll be sending in a report,' he frowned, 'but I can tell you I smell a rat here, madam.'

In fact he was hopping mad because he had wanted to find something wrong but the children had answered all the questions correctly.

'It's just too perfect – every child has given me a copy-book answer. I wouldn't be surprised if you've cheated again, Miss Manning-Smythe. You are already suspected of tampering with your exam results. There's no way children can be as knowledgeable as this with only three days' school work a week. The sums just don't add up!'

Potty Smythe was furious with this repellent little man. She would have liked to deal him a good near-side forehand with her father's old polo stick which was mounted in a glass case above the filing cabinet!

'Dr Swottworm,' she replied as calmly as possible, 'that is because our children at Fetlocks Hall are very quick learners, as you can see. There would certainly be no need to tamper with their exam results.'

Swottworm went a horrible shade of purple.

'There's one way of proving my suspicions are correct,' he raged. 'I insist you put a team forward for the first round of my new inter-school "Brainstorm" competition and there's absolutely no time for any preparation. Your team will have to perform at 10 a.m. tomorrow morning against St Custard's School for the Superintelligent, the cleverest school in Europe. The quiz will take place in Bournemouth at St Custard's. The questions will be set by an anonymous question master which are of his or her choice on their own subjects. Not even I know what they will be.'

Potty Smythe was lost for words. This was so unfair. The Health and Safety inspectors were due tomorrow as well at 2 p.m. It would take at least an hour to get to Bournemouth and another hour for their return journey, leaving little or no time to get things ship-shape for the next OGRIBS invasion! Although there was little chance of beating the famous St Custard's, Potty Smythe had every faith that Penny would come up with something.

She mustered all her courage and calmly replied, 'We'll be there.'

Swottworm told her not to trouble to show him out. He marched from the room, not even bothering to close the door behind him.

Two minutes later there was a ghastly scream and a terrible clanking noise.

Potty ran out on to the landing and peered over the banisters to the great hall below.

Swottworm was crashing around the walls with the helmet and visor (firmly shut) from Sir Walter's suit of armour stuck to his head!

Arabella and Antonia were sitting on the banisters literally laughing their heads off!

Doubled over with laughter, Potty Smythe rang Sidney Sidewinder the janitor, who turned up with his box of spanners. It took him an hour to unscrew the helmet's ancient bolts. Swottworm's head emerged with a huge red bulbous nose which had become stuck in the visor when the twins had rammed the helmet on him.

Mrs Dogberry asked if he'd like a nice raw piece of venison steak from the kitchen to reduce the swelling but he'd had enough of Fetlocks Hall by then and couldn't wait to get back to Bournemouth. He bundled himself and his nose back into the bug-like car and sped down the drive as fast as it could go.

The twins had overheard the conversation between Potty Smythe and Dr Swottworm.

They floated into the Computer Studies room, where Penny was playing a game of digital chess with Gig, and told them the devastating news.

Gig offered to help but couldn't find anything out this time except that the quiz questions had to be set by the question master, handwritten and kept in a secret place until moments before the competition.

Penny and the twins went back to H.Q. to tell Potty Smythe, who shook her head and said, 'This is really going to be difficult but I know Fetlocks Hall will do its best. We'll just have to take pot luck and bite the bullet.'

Penny desperately needed help from the rest of the Flyers. She managed to round everybody up later that day in the library.

'If we don't beat St Custard's and pass the Health and Safety test all in one day,' she told them, 'OGRIBS will impose restrictions on the school and bring us into line with ordinary boarding schools. That means more school work and less time for ponies. Probably only one hour's riding a week to be exact like most other pony schools!'

'That's out of the question!' said Dom.

'We'll fight to the end for our ponies!' said Sam.

'Take the man!' shouted Carlos in polo talk.

'Doom to St Custard's!' yelled Pip.

Matt said something quietly in Arabic.

'It means "He who dares, wins",' he explained.

'AND WE DARE, DON'T WE?' added Penny, standing with her hands on her hips.

They all agreed to volunteer to represent the

school for the quiz team even if they had to swot all night.

Potty Smythe was overwhelmed with admiration for them.

'It's so brave of you to offer,' she said when they all piled into the study to tell her. 'But it's best you children get a good night's rest. It's going to be sticky going tomorrow, chaps. If only we knew who the question master was we'd have some idea of what they were likely to ask as the questions will be related to their own interests but Swottworm's got that under wraps as well.'

The Fetlocks Hall Flyers took their headmistress's advice and went to bed early but everyone was too anxious to sleep much.

CHAPTER NINE

Quizzical Custard

The next day the teachers set up one of the two Fetlocks Hall horseboxes as a mobile learning centre. They loaded computers, files, reference books on all kinds of subjects, pens, paper and Ethelene Giggabit for extra measure into one with the Fetlocks Hall Flyers team. The other horsebox was stuffed with pupils who were coming along as supporters. Henry drove the leading lorry with Ben following behind with the other. Potty Smythe sat in the front with Henry, giving directions to Bournemouth. The Fitznicely twins, unseen by anyone else except the headmistress and Penny, reclined in the space on top of the driver's cab on a bunk. They had not only come as supporters but were looking for a chance to play another trick on Swottworm since their last one had been such a hoot.

The lorries set off at 6 a.m. because Bournemouth is a busy town and they did not want to get stuck in the rush hour. The teachers coached the team as much as they could all the way there, using the equipment they had brought with them. The time seemed to go very quickly. Soon they had left the town centre and were climbing a hill which led to St Custard's school.

Swottworm was waiting in the reception area of the big ugly red-brick building.

'So this is your team, Miss Manning-Smythe,' he said sarcastically, picking a bit of straw out of Penny's plaits.

'We're all very excited about the quiz,' said Sam bravely. 'Thank you so much for inviting us.'

'We're going to pulverise the Custards,' said Pip.

Potty Smythe gave her an unseen nudge.

'Such enthusiasm!' she said. 'Please forgive them, Dr Swottworm.'

Antonia and Arabella had disappeared. Penny

had no idea where they had gone. The team filed into the St Custard's Assembly Hall which was already packed with a large audience. The stage was set out with two panels for six contestants, one for each school.

Between the panels, in front of some purple curtains, was a lectern for the surprise question master to read from.

The audience were seated and the teams took their places on the stage.

The Custards looked very slick in their yellow blazers with red binding. There were four girls and two boys, one of them with horrible spots and another with braces on his teeth.

As Penny sat down with the rest of her team, Arabella and Antonia floated up through the stage floor like a pair of genies.

'You wait and see who's asking the questions,' they beamed. '*And* we've got Swottworm again!'

With that they faded back into the floor.

The lights dimmed and Swottworm stepped into the spotlight.

'Ladies and gentlemen, pupils and teachers,' he began, 'welcome to the first round of "Brainstorm", a new inter-school quiz sponsored by OGRIBS to find the cleverest school in the country. On my left we have St Custard's School for the Superintelligent and on my right we have Fetlocks Hall.

'And our mystery question master tonight is . . .' (Here he turned to face the purple curtains, revealing the big hole Arabella and Antonia had cut in the seat of his trousers showing his baggy underpants.)

The audience roared with laughter. The spotlight moved from the underpants to the curtains, which moved to the side.

'Dame Gilly Jumpwell, OBE!' continued a rather perplexed Swottworm.

The laughing gave way to applause as Gilly stepped on to the stage holding a folder which she placed on the lectern.

Potty Smythe fell off her chair with a bump. She couldn't believe her luck! It was none other than her old pony club friend and International Event legend Gilly, who had already been down to Fetlocks Hall to teach the children eventing. She had forgotten her old chum was not only a fellow of the British Horse Society but a fellow of Cambridge University and one of the cleverest women in the world!

Penny and the rest of the Flyers looked at each other and beamed.

After more applause for Gilly the lights went up and she gave a short speech.

'Thank you, ladies and gentleman,' she smiled. 'I have been asked by OGRIBS to set questions relating to my own subject. Good luck, everyone. Here is my first question, which is on science and goes to St Custard's. What is the sensitive laminae?'

There was complete silence from St Custard's for a moment and then they whispered together. Eventually the spotty boy piped up with, 'A black hole in space.'

'Sorry, St Custard's, that is the wrong answer,' smiled Gilly. 'I offer this question to Fetlocks Hall.'

Penny pushed her buzzer. 'It's a spongy mass of blood vessels supporting the pedal bone in the hoof of a horse,' she answered.

'Correct answer, Fetlocks. You get a point and the next question,' said Gilly. 'In English literature, who is said to be the "fine lady" referred to in the nursery rhyme "Ride a cock horse to Banbury Cross/To see a fine lady upon a white horse"?'

Penny did not know the answer to this one so conferred with the others. They did not know either so Dom said, 'Let's hazard a guess at Queen Elizabeth the First.'

'Well done again, Fetlocks Hall,' said Gilly with a twinkle in her bright blue eyes. 'Absolutely right. You get another point and the next question.

In computer science, what is a Trojan Horse Program?'

Nobody knew at all. Gig was jumping up in her seat in the audience but she was forbidden to help them. Pip suggested they guess it was a DVD on Greek Mythology.

Gilly looked downcast as she told them that was the wrong answer. She offered the question to St Custard's, who got it right.

'It's a virus,' said a tall thin blonde girl with oblong-shaped black-rimmed glasses.

Gilly had to admit that this was the correct answer and awarded them a point and offered them the next question.

'In biology,' she said, 'what is the scientific name for the common horse chestnut tree?'

The small St Custard's boy with braces came up with the right answer,

'*Hippocastanum vulgare*,' he lisped.

The Fetlocks team were getting worried now. St Custard's seemed to be on a roll. If they won it would mean the end of Fetlocks Hall as the magical pony school it was!

'OK, St Custard's,' said Gilly, swallowing hard. 'You get the next question. In Greek mythology, who sprang from the neck of Medusa when she was beheaded?'

A red-headed girl with freckles rang her bell and said, 'Poseidon.'

Gilly inwardly gave a sigh of relief and told her she was wrong, offering the question and the point to Fetlocks. Penny buzzed in with the right answer immediately. As she was constantly in touch with winged horses she knew she was correct.

'Pegasus, the winged horse god,' she said.

Everybody was relieved but it was not over yet. Fetlocks was in the lead with one question to go – they simply had to get it right. Potty Smythe was poised on the edge of her chair.

'Fetlocks Hall gets the point and the next question,' said Gilly slowly. 'In History, when did Lady Godiva ride through the streets of Coventry? Was it nine hundred years ago, one hundred years ago or twenty-five years ago?'

This was a tricky question as well.

'It can't have been twenty-five years ago,' said Matt, 'or she would have been arrested.'

Carlos said that the story was much older than a hundred years.

'Nine hundred years!' cried Sam at the last second.

'Right again, Fetlocks,' beamed Gilly. 'That concludes my questions for this round of "Brainstorm" and the winners are Fetlocks Hall with four points.

Well done, Fetlocks! Please give a big hand to our losers, St Custard's, with two points.'

The Flyers went mad. They could not believe their luck! Their supporters and Potty Smythe threw their hats into the air, waved hockey sticks, cracked hunting whips and sent up a wild view holla. There could be no doubt that the Flyers had saved the school by beating St Custard's and swatting Swottworm's quiz.

'Come on,' shouted Henry, 'let's get on the lorries. We've got to get back to Fetlocks by 2 p.m.!'

They all rushed for the door. Swottworm was furious. He chased after them but Antonia and Arabella weren't finished with him yet. They cut his braces, and what was left of his trousers slipped to his feet. He fell over and tumbled though a door marked 'Ladies' Toilet', where several very offended elderly ladies beat him up with their handbags.

Everyone piled on to the lorries which hurtled out of the St Custard's gates and made for the main road back to West Dorset. They simply had to make it home for the visit from Dr Meena Sweepover and Nigel Snoop from Health and Safety.

Potty Smythe didn't think it would be a good idea to greet her old friend Gilly at the quiz. However, she decided she'd definitely phone and thank her when all this was over.

CHAPTER TEN

The Curse Lifted

The traffic was awful on the way out of Bournemouth. Ben and Henry were tearing their hair out. They came to a road sign that said 'Diversion' and had to drive halfway around the town before they got on to the right road for Dorchester. Potty Smythe was pretty sure she'd seen Swottworm's little green bug of a car parked behind the sign.

'So that's his plan,' she said to Henry. 'He failed to get his way because our students were cleverer than he thought so now he's moved the diversion sign to make us late so that the next inspectors think we have something to hide!'

Ben and Henry drove as fast as the lorries could go but they only screamed in through the school gates at 2.30 p.m.!

'We're sunk!' exclaimed Potty, seeing an official-looking car parked by the front steps.

'No, we're not!' cried Penny, pointing across the lawn to the Ladies' Garden, where Countess Mortia with her two children by her side was serving 'orange juice' to the two inspectors.

Henry stopped the lorry and let Potty Smythe and Penny out. They ran across the lawn to join the little group in the garden.

'Ah, so pleased to meet you, Miss Manning-Smythe,' grinned Dr Sweepover, turning towards her with a glass of Fangley Zest in her hand. 'I must congratulate you on your excellent home-grown blood orange juice.'

'It is quite perfection,' agreed Nigel Snoop, showing small sharp teeth on either side of his grin. Both inspectors seemed to be turning paler with each sip as Countess Mortia, Merc and Morri ladled more of the stuff into their glasses. The Fangley Zest seemed to be working with great effect!

'Look,' said Morri, 'it's Daddy. He's back!'

Penny followed his gaze towards the tall pretty archway of red roses to the east of the garden. Two large pony Veggipires were hanging upside down in it.

Pruning the roses to one side of the archway, wearing a large straw hat and sunglasses, was Uncle Faustus.

He strode over and the Countess introduced her husband to her new converts.

'I'm so pleased you are enjoying my orange cocktail,' he said, shaking their now long thin hands. 'Do come and meet some little pets of mine.' He beckoned to the pony Veggipires, who flopped down on the grass beside the inspectors.

'Oh, aren't they sweet,' cooed Dr Meena, stroking one on the head.

'Would you like to ride them?' he asked.

The inspectors were overjoyed at the invitation. They chose one each and climbed on to their backs.

Slowly the pony Veggipires rose into the air.

Dr Meena and Nigel Snoop giggled with joy as they flew around the lawn.

Hardly anyone could stand up for laughing.

'They make very good Veggipires, thanks to my Fangley Zest, though I say it myself,' said Uncle Faustus, 'and it's all thanks to you, Penny, that the Curse of the Pony Vampires is history.'

After their ride Potty Smythe took the Health and Safety inspectors on a tour of the school. Now that they were eccentric Veggipires, they loved old Mr Pennypot's leech farm in the swimming pool and congratulated him on the work the leeches were doing at the local hospital. They adored Mrs Honeybun's ancient kitchen and were delighted with her gift of deliciously dirty organic home-grown vegetables. They enthused over the crumbling plaster, draughty windows and untidy dormitories of Fetlocks Hall. They especially liked the pony Veggipires and were over the moon when Uncle Faustus said they could keep them!

Dr Meena and Nigel Snoop assured Potty Smythe that there was no school safer and healthier than Fetlocks in their view and that they would write a glowing report on their inspection for OGRIBS.

Uncle Faustus suggested that they fly their new pets home. Sidney Sidewinder would deliver their car later.

The inspectors thought this was a wonderful idea. They climbed on to the pony Veggipires' backs and rose into the sky. Smiling toothy grins, they waved goodbye as they flew away over the park's great oak trees. Everybody burst out laughing.

'Well,' said Penny. 'Swottworm is swatted, Dr

Meena and Nigel Snoop are delighted with our Health and Safety at Fetlocks, and the Curse of the Pony Vampires is lifted. Come on, Merc and Morri — let's find the others. There's time for a few chukkas.'

Merc and Morri asked their mother and father if they would like to watch the game.

'We've been invited to play croquet with Sir Walter and Lady Sarah,' replied the Countess, 'but do run along and have fun, darlings. We will tell each other about our separate games later.'

After an exciting match where the girls' polo team won thanks to Merc's six goals, Penny rode Patch back to the orchard. As the golden sun was dipping down to the sea on the distant horizon there was a sudden green flash. Penny could make out the shape of King Valentine Silverwings flying towards her. He landed gracefully and trotted up to the little girl and her pony.

'It's all OK now, Your Majesty,' she said. 'The Devliped threat is over and Fetlocks Hall is back to normal.'

'I knew I could count on you, Princess Penny,' he smiled as she and Patch walked by his side into the twilight.

The end and a new beginning

Read on for Chapter 1 of Penny's
next exciting adventure

The Enchanted Pony

CHAPTER ONE

A Mixed Blessing

'Parents,' sighed Portia Manning-Smythe, head-mistress of Fetlocks Hall Pony School, 'can be a mixed blessing!'

She had just finished a telephone call from Mr and Mrs Simms about their daughter, Penny. They were concerned that her letters and emails home seemed to be full of ponies and nothing to do with any school work. Potty Smythe had reassured them that Penny was doing extremely well at her lessons and that she had probably thought school work was very matter-of-fact and not necessary to mention in her letters. Ponies, on the other hand, are much more exciting to a ten-year-old pony-mad little girl, so naturally she'd want to tell her parents all about her adventures with them.

Mr and Mrs Simms had *no* idea what sort of adventures Penny was having at this very unusual pony school, where extraordinary things happen. In fact, Penny was not only an exceptionally talented horsewoman, but just happened to be the hundredth Unicorn Princess of Equitopia, the Kingdom of the Unicorns. She possessed magical pony powers and was a very important child indeed! She'd ONLY saved Equitopia and Terrestequinus (our planet) from invasion by the wicked Devlipeds. If those nasty, fire-breathing, scaly little red ponies had gained control of these two worlds they would have made life extremely unpleasant for all of us!

Fetlocks Hall had a very important role to play in Equitopia. Its main task was to find and educate very special equichildren who might one day become A students at the school. On reaching this level, pupils can receive magical powers similar to Penny's. While the unicorns are responsible for keeping the mythical scales called the Equilibrium of Goodness balanced in favour of good, the wicked Devlipeds are always plotting to steal them. Their plan is to tip the balance towards evil so that they can make the two worlds as nasty as their own. A students have the power to assist the reigning Unicorn Princess to protect the scales, and therefore keep Equitopia and Terrestequinus safe.

This, of course, was S.U.S. (Secret Unicorn Society) business and that was highly secret. Parents, unless they themselves were past Fetlocks A students, could never be told about the other-worldly side of Fetlocks Hall.

Potty Smythe smiled to herself and took a gulp of tea from her favourite tin mug.

'. . . And her parents want to know how Penny's doing at computer studies!' she giggled.

It had been predicted by Valentine Silverwings, King of the Unicorns, that Penny would come to Fetlocks Hall. He had given her certain magical gifts which she had earned at her coronation by passing some very rigorous and scary tests. The Lance of Courage protected her against all evil, the Vial of Unicorn Tears helped her to heal all wounds and ill-nesses, and Queen Starlight's Horn, with its magical music, tamed any wild beast or monster. There was no way Penny or Potty Smythe could share this information with *ordinary* mortals because it was S.U.S. business, but they could tell their extraordinary friends, the Fitznicely family – Lady Sarah, Sir Walter and their mischievous twin daughters, Arabella and Antonia, who were the resident ghosts at Fetlocks Hall. They were all former unicorn royalty and they helped Penny rule as current Unicorn Princess.

Her *everyday* life was supported by her fab chums and teammates, The Fetlocks Hall Flyers, Sam, Pip, Dom, Carlos and Matt. Recently two new pupils had joined the crew. Morri and Merc were the Veggipire children of Lady Mortia-Antoinette and Sir Faustus Fangley-Fitznicely, the unusual inhabitants from the Dower House in the woods near Fetlocks Hall. They were actually hundreds of years old but being Veggipires they could be whatever age they wanted. They'd chosen to be twelve and thirteen years old. *They* knew Penny was a Unicorn Princess but kept the Equitopian secret safe as Penny did theirs. The other children and their parents had no idea that the Fangley-Fitznicelys could turn into bats whenever they liked!

Potty Smythe sighed as she sorted through a huge pile of letters on her desk from pupils' mothers and fathers who, like Penny's, seemed to be feeling left out of their children's school life.

Mr and Mrs Goodfellow had written to say they were worried about their daughter Stephanie, who had asked if she could stay at Fetlocks during the school holidays instead of coming home at all!

Tumbleweed, the little Exmoor pony belonging to Susie Hamilton's parents, hated leaving the school at the end of term so much he refused to go into his trailer. Even Penny, who had the magical gift of Equalese, enabling her to talk to ponies, could not persuade him.

The Waterford family from Ireland were concerned that their son's pony, Coolin, was not jumping as well as expected. Potty Smythe knew how she could solve that problem. She'd get Penny to jump him for Seamus because one of the special gifts King Valentine had given her was the art of Equibatics. She could actually fly ponies, so jumping was no problem.

Herr Klimt, one of the most ambitious parents, was moaning because his daughter's pony was not getting good enough marks in his freestyle dressage to music. Penny, however, had already spoken to the little German pony and discovered that he hated the music and found it too difficult to change legs to the beat. Penny possessed the gift of Equiballet and could make ponies dance. She and Rheingold worked out a new routine to different music. The result was that Potty Smythe received another letter a few weeks later from Herr Klimt, enclosing a cheque to pay for a much-needed new dressage arena.

Although parents were very important as they paid fees to keep the school going, Potty Smythe also wanted to keep relatives happy and informed of their children's school progress. This was all very well but there were other important things for her to do at Fetlocks Hall, like keeping out Devlipeds, finding enough money to run the place and stopping the authorities closing it down! But school fees and new parents were always needed, so something extra had to be done to keep the present parents happy and attract others with the kind of children Fetlocks needed. She decided to hold a staff meeting to see if any of the teachers could come up with a clever idea as to how this could be done.

They all met up next Monday morning in H.Q. (the headmistress's study).

'What about an emailed newsletter at the end of each term?' said Quentin Theary from Physics.

'Or a parent–teacher association with monthly meetings?' suggested Miss Mappit, the geography teacher.

These and similar suggestions seemed good ideas

but Potty Smythe was looking for something more spectacular that could attract new parents as well.

The teachers were all sitting round scratching their heads when Potty's two deerhounds ran over to the balcony window and wagged their tails. They had noticed Penny flying her best pony friend, Patch, around the park. Of course no one else could see this as Penny was invisible when Equibatic to anyone except Potty, the Fitznicely family, ponies, dogs, unicorns and Devlipeds.

'I bet I know someone who could come up with the answer,' thought Potty Smythe, reversing towards the window and giving Penny the secret 'both thumbs up' sign behind her back, indicating that she needed to talk to her.

On her second lap of the great house Penny noticed the signal and landed Patch at the front of the Hall. She slipped off his brown and white back, gave him a pat and raced up the stone steps to the main entrance. Her magical gifts were hidden under the third step and guarded by two stone unicorns on either side. As she dashed past they saluted her with the usual rainbow of stars from their eyes.

'Thanks, Hippolita and Rain,' said Penny in Equalese.

Moments later Penny knocked on the door of H.Q. Potty Smythe opened it and invited her inside.

'Ah, Penny,' she said with a wink and a smile, 'come to fetch those new pony magazines for the library, have you? There they are, on my desk.'

'Of course, Miss,' said Penny with a smile, picking up the bundle. 'Will there be anything else I can do?'

'Well,' continued the headmistress, 'we were all trying to think of a way of getting parents involved in the school a little more. As a Fetlocks student, what do you think your own people would like?'

'That's easy,' said Penny. 'How about a parents' day where we can all show off what we have learned – and the ponies, of course. Something like a county show or country fair.'

'Excellent idea!' cried the headmistress, turning to her astonished staff, who were staring over their tea-cups. Everyone agreed it was a brilliant thought.

'Thank you, Penny,' grinned Potty Smythe. 'Now run along with those . . . and by the way, Patch is eating the petunias.'